We Are Writers!

CHERRY TREE PRIMARY SCHOOL

An Introduction by Michael Rosen

Writing down what we think and feel is a great way to remember things and a great way to share with others the things we care about.

Once you write something down, you've recorded it—just as we do when we take photos. This means we can go back to it again and again and think about it, almost as if it's not you who wrote it. Well, in a way, it isn't. It's the person you were when you wrote it! So the first person you share writing with is you. This means you can judge yourself and think about what kind of person you are or were. Then, if there are people out there who are going to read what you wrote, that's great too. What you wrote about becomes part of the way we all find out together what matters and what the possible ways to behave, think and feel about things are.

Michael Rosen
Children's Laureate 2007–2009

Published by Scholastic Ltd for

Cherry Tree Primary School
Hardy Road
Lymm
Cheshire
WA13 0NX

First published in Great Britain in 2020

Printed and bound by CPI Group (UK) Ltd, Croydon, CR0 4YY

Foreword

When 2020 began, we were unaware of how events were going to unfold, not just in the UK but globally too. We had no idea that we were about to be challenged in a way we had never known before.

Most of our children started the year not knowing the words pandemic, hand-sanitiser, unprecedented or coronavirus. Covid-19 began to spread and our vocabulary was soon to change.

Many of the goals, resolutions and plans made at the start of the year have understandably been cancelled or postponed. As a nation, we like to plan ahead, maybe book a holiday or arrange a birthday party. As more and more events had to be cancelled the ever-changing situation was unsettling for everyone.

However, lockdown wasn't all 'doom and gloom'. Staying at home brought us time to reflect; to consider what was really important in our lives; and to learn from our children. We began to spend more time in the 'great outdoors' and our carbon footprints rapidly reduced.

Fortunately, we had some of the best weather I have ever known during the spring and summer of 2020. The sunshine lifted our spirits as we attempted to maintain some form of normality.

The children of Cherry Tree have been with us every step and I am eternally grateful to have been able to continue working in school, throughout the lockdown. Initially, only children of keyworkers came to school. In June three year groups could return to school and in September we were fully open again.

What an absolute privilege it has been for all of us at Cherry Tree to support the children in their journey through 2020. They have given us meaning and purpose at a time when the virus felt all-consuming. Our children have continued to embody our core values: to be happy, resilient, compassionate, open-minded, aspirational and independent.

This unique book captures the children's thoughts and reflections on a year that none of us will ever forget. Every child in school in the Autumn Term of 2020 is represented within these pages. I hope you enjoy reading about this year, through the eyes of our lovely children.

With all my very best wishes,

Helen Graham

Contents

Class 2 60

My Lockdown Memories

Noah Antrobus Class F

I enjoyed doing assault courses in the garden with my big sister Holly and playing with our new beagle puppy called Everest.

My Lockdown Memories

Jack Boden Class F

I liked making brownies with mummy and painting rainbows. We clapped outside for the nurses and doctors.

My Lockdown Memories

Louie Boden Class F

I stayed with my grandparents for 8 weeks at the start of lock down. I had an amazing time building with my lego, going on my bike, baking cakes and making experiments with my aunty. I missed my usual routine but missed my mummy and daddy the most.

My Lockdown

Harry Chorlton   Class F

I made cakes with Grace and Daddy. We made them for Grandma. All my family played in the paddling pool. I stood on the chair and looked into next-door's garden, it's a bit smaller than my garden. I went for a walk with Mummy.

My Lockdown Memories

Freddie Clarkendale Class F

I really missed my Popsy during lockdown and my friends. But I loved spending lots of time with my mummy and sister and I loved the really big chalk drawing we did on the pavement outside! It was a really long road that had lots of buildings such as a post office and petrol station and police station!

My Lockdown Memories

Ava Dean Class F

I liked that my daddy was working from home. At lunch we would all have a picnic in the garden every day. Mummy would take me and my baby brother on a walk every day and we would search for Lymm rocks. I did miss my grandmas and grandads.

My Lockdown Journey

Louis Frizelle Class F

I played at nursery. I was sad because I couldn't go on holiday. I could still go to my Grandma and Grandad's.

My Lockdown Memories

Emma Gallagher Class F

I remember doing my threading and hanging it up. I liked playing with Katie and Alex and catching frogs together. We all went on the trampoline. Gallagher Tree School was fun and Katie and Alex were there with me every day. Mummy was my teacher and we did spellings. I made potions in the garden. We had lots of barbecues with Mummy and Daddy. We all walked Hoopy in Spud Wood. I loved being at home with everyone!

My Lockdown Journey

Holly Grainge Class F

I enjoyed baking cakes and cookies (and eating them). I enjoyed playing outside in the garden and playing in the paddling pool when it was sunny. I liked going for late night walks, but I really missed seeing my Nanna and Grandad.

My Lockdown Memories

Annabelle Guthrie Class F

I liked watching Joe Wicks on the TV and jumping up and down with my brother. I missed all my friends at nursery.

My Lockdown Memories

Dexter Horner Class F

During lockdown I missed seeing my cousin Teddy. Sometimes I face timed him. I did lots of Joe Wicks and 'Draw with Rob'. I liked doing baking and science experiments. We went for lots of walks and I got much better at riding my bike. I loved riding round the garden on the go kart and doing front flips on the trampoline. I played and played and played with my brother and sisters

My Lockdown Memory

Penny Howarth Class F

I enjoyed camping in the garden, lots of baking, rainbow crafts, PE with Joe Wicks, lots of walks and learning to ride my bike without stabilisers!

My Lockdown Memories

Alfie Klendjian Class F

I missed my friends at nursery but loved it when we put our big tent up in the back garden. It stayed up for 9 weeks and we slept in it when the weather was nice. Our cat Mozart sometimes came in and slept with us too, which I loved.

My Lockdown Memories

Ben Klendjian Class F

I missed my friends but enjoyed doing baking - we made flapjacks. I also liked the day the ice cream van came right to our house and I could have whatever I wanted.

My Lockdown Memories

Olivia Knowles Class F

I don't like the virus because my friends cannot come to my Halloween party and they cannot Trick or Treat at my house.

My Lockdown Memories

Phoebe Lee Class F

I was sad because I missed my friends at school but we did see each other through the computer and I talked to my teachers on the phone every week.

My Lockdown Memories

Scarlett Lee Class F

I liked being at home and playing in the garden, especially splashing in the paddling pool with my big sister. I liked finding new walks around Lymm and cycling along the TPT. I liked our VE Day street party in May.

I missed my friends at nursery and I missed being able to see my family (grandparents and cousins). I missed my swimming lessons and dance class.

My Lockdown Memories

Alfie Linderman Class F

I didn't like not being able to see my Nannas and Grandad or my aunties and uncles during lockdown. I also missed my friends from nursery a lot and I didn't understand why Mummy was now working from home but couldn't play with me all day and instead had to do work on her laptop. Daddy also broke his leg at the start of lockdown which wasn't fun! But I loved all the times we played in the garden and had lots of water fights with Mummy and Daddy and played in the paddling pool. I also enjoyed making a Star Wars Easter bonnet with Mummy and doing an Easter egg hunt in the garden! I also enjoyed our walks to Lymm Dam collecting pine cones, conkers and leaves.As there was no nursery or school, each night, Mummy & Daddy and I would sit curled up on the couch and watch a family film together.

My Lockdown

Joseph Osborne Class F

Mummy and Daddy put a fence up. I played games in the front garden. I liked playing Snakes and Ladders with Mummy.

Lockdown

Ben Peers Class F

I remember baking lots of cakes and playing with my brother Josh. Every day at bedtime Josh and I asked for a bunk bed so we could share a room. During lockdown we just moved our mattresses into the same room and as soon as the shops opened we bought a bunk bed. Each night I asked if Peppa Pig World was open yet as we had planned to go. Finally in the summer we went there and it was great!

My Lockdown

Mia Pink Class F

I didn't like not going to the park and seeing all my friends, but I did like staying with my Mum. We did some rainbow pictures.

My Lockdown

Morgan Roberts Class F

I made cupcakes with my sister. I played a game where you tried to solve things and you got a sweet. Seren got more sweets than me.

My Lockdown Memories

Hugo Robinson Class F

I missed my friends at preschool and being able to see my cousins, Tilly, Charlie and Penny. I enjoyed painting, making bread, banana cake and fruit salads. I loved playing with Toby in the garden, particularly when it was hot and we could play in the paddling pool! It was Toby's birthday in lockdown, so we had a Super Mario cake and built a den in the lounge, which Toby and I slept in!

My Lockdown

Carter Samuels-Camozzi Class F

I made cakes with Dad and played Snakes and Ladders with Daddy.

My Lockdown Memories

Ida Stewart Class F

I enjoyed bike rides on the Trans-pennine trail on my trailer bike with Mummy and Sullivan. I did Cosmic Yoga and Joe Wicks but I missed my friends Olivia and Emma from preschool.

My Lockdown

Gabriella Stockton Class F

I went in the paddling pool. I played monsters with Daddy and went for walks. I went on the slide as well.

My Lockdown Memories

Alex Stroud Class F

I liked having the paddling pool in the garden and playing cricket with Mummy, Daddy and Joshua. But I was sad that Nana couldn't come round because of the germs

My Lockdown Memories

Rosie Wardle Class F

I liked it when my brother Matthew pretended to be my teacher and we did school every morning. I liked that he was here and I hugged him.

My Lockdown Memories

Harriet Woods Class F

I missed all my friends at pre school and seeing my grandparents and cousins. I liked doing baking, crafts, playing in the garden and paddling pool and having walks in the country.

My Lockdown Acrostic Poem

Libby Allan Class 1

F amily played with me
A slide in my back garden
M y mum watches TV with me
I love my mum
L ittle house full of toys
Y our mum cooks food

My Lockdown Acrostic Poem

Grace Allsop Class 1

F un time with my mum
A ria is my friend
M y mum is the best because she gives me
milk
I sabelle and me saved a worm and it was
shivering with cold
L ibby is the best friend
Y ou love me to the moon and back

My Acrostic Lockdown Poem

Harvey Appleton Class 1

F un times in my garden
A must have - a good time in my playroom
M um hugs me when I get up
I n lockdown I made cookie dough mix
L etting my dog out, playing football
Y ou always love me

My Lockdown Acrostic Poem

Harry Bett Class 1

F amily is fantastic
A parcel came to my house
M ummy played games with me
I got a sword
L ovely lie in
Y ummy food

My Lockdown Acrostic Poem

Mason Broomfield Class 1

F our people in my family, daddy, mummy,
Lincon and Mason.
A family. They give me food to eat.
M mm that was yummy.
I go to bed when I'm sleepy.
L ove my family.
Y ou play video games with me.

My Lockdown Acrostic Poem

Grace Caton Class 1

F un is for friends and family
A t home I had fun
M y best friends like to play
I n lockdown I did a lot of playing
L oving cuddles on the sofa
Y ou can play with me

My Lockdown Acrostic Poem

Oscar Dempsey Class 1

F amily went on walks
A frog jumped out of our fence
M y dad took me to the shop
I was playing with Lego
L ove my mum
Y ou did some cooking

My Lockdown Acrostic Poem

Emmie Edwards Class 1

F un with dad
A mazing time at home
M um is super
I love my mum so much
L ove my mum
Y ummy dinners

My Lockdown Acrostic Poem

Henry Guthrie Class 1

F un playing cricket
A nnabelle is the best
M ummy makes cakes
I explore with Daddy
L ove yo-yos
Y es, Henry is the best

My Lockdown Acrostic Poem

Teddy Hopkin Class 1

F un times
A t home I did some craft
M y mum is the best
I slept in my bed
L ots of playing
Y ou and me play

My Lockdown Acrostic Poem

Logan Jackson-Kenway Class 1

F un with family
A pplause NHS
M ummy
I played with Daddy
L ots of games
Y ummy cakes

My Lockdown Acrostic Poem

Philip Ktistis Class 1

F un with Alex
A pplause the NHS
M y mum playing with me
I ride my bike
L ovely sunshine
Y ummy cakes

My Lockdown Acrostic Poem

Elsie Lord Class 1

F abulous dad and mum
A lot of work
M y mummy and daddy played with me
I rode my bike
L ove you so much
Y ou will have fun

My Lockdown Acrostic Poem

Jake Lubbock Class 1

F amily and I played in my bedroom
A parcel came for my mum
M um got me some chocolate
I had some movie nights
L ego is fun
Y ou had a phone call

My Lockdown Acrostic Poem

Emily Mayne Class 1

F un with mum and dad
A mazing dad because he took me out on my
  bike
M cDonalds with mum
I love my mum
L etting my dog out
Y ou do gymnastics

My Lockdown Acrostic Poem

Iseabal Morrison Class 1

F amily time together
A t home I played with Lego by myself
M y family went to my Papa's farm
I played on my Ipad
L ots of time spent together
Y ou can make my bed

My Lockdown Acrostic Poem

Finlay Murphy Class 1

F un times at the park
A t home everyone ate pizza
M e and mummy wasn't nervous
I went to swimming
L ots of time going to the park
Y ou and me eating popcorn

My Lockdown Acrostic Poem

Aria Naylor Class 1

F amily time was amazing
A pril was Sofia's birthday
M y mummy cooked food
I played with my teddies
L ucia helped me when I was hurt
Y ou love me

My Lockdown Acrostic Poem

Jessica O'Leary Class 1

F un times
A little girl found me
M y mum helps me
I am Jessica
L ots of time being at the park
Y ou love me

My Lockdown Acrostic Poem

Verity Pridding Class 1

F abulous mum
A mazing nurses
M y rabbit is a boy
I ride my bike
L ovely daddy
Y ummy cakes

My Lockdown Acrostic Poem

Kishan Rao Class 1

F un is for friends and family
A t home I had fun
M y best friends like to play
I n the lockdown I did a lot of playing
L oving cuddles on the sofa
Y ou can play with me

My Lockdown Acrostic Poem

Joseph Sharples Class 1

F amily is fun
A big parcel came to my house
M um did some cooking
I played with my toys
L ego is fun to play with
Y ou had a zoom chat

My Acrostic Lockdown Poem

Jeevay Sidhu Class 1

F antastic dad took me to the park
A ll the grown-ups had to wear masks
M y mummy worked in a pharmacy during
lockdown
I played in the garden
L atest news said that everyone had to stay at
home
Y ou (Biraj) and me were best friends

My Lockdown Acrostic Poem

Anika Singh Class 1

F un with family
A mazing nurses
M ummy made yummy food
I n the park
L ots of TV
Y ummy chips

My Lockdown Acrostic Poem

Adanna Swan-Wolffe Class 1

F un times at home
A t home with mom and dad
M y lovely mom
I n the garden with dad
L ove my family
Y ou and me at home

My Lockdown Acrostic Poem

Amy Swettenham Class 1

F un times when the plants grew and I could
pick them
A t home my mum helped me make cakes
with chocolate sauce
M y sister and me played with ponies and
unicorns
I played on the trampoline, it was super
bouncy
L uke was in the bath and I wanted to play
with him
Y our favourite book - 'I need a wee!'

My Lockdown Acrostic Poem

Alfie Trippett Class 1

F un with family
Amazing NHS
M unching cakes
I n the garden
L ots of sunshine
Y ummy chips

My Lockdown Acrostic Poem

Henry Watson Class 1

F amily is kind
A mazing mum gave me a car
M um gave me toys
I did running
L ove - my mum loves me
Y ummy food

My Lockdown Acrostic Poem

Esme Wee Class 1

F un toad in my garden
A frog went in my garden
M y sister had some ice cream
I did some art
L ots of fun at home
Y ummy cakes I love

My Lockdown Acrostic Poem

Isabelle Wright Class 1

F amily can't go into peoples houses
A nother hour in bed
M y mum can't go into work
I did playing in my bedroom
L ove my mum
Y um yum, I had ice cream

My Lockdown Memories

Natalie Agamian Class 2

In lockdown I went to Scotland and there was a big hill. Me and Arthur rolled down the hill. At night we had two hot chocolates and rolled down the big hill. It was fun. We stayed in a little cottage and for breakfast we had waffles with chocolate spread on. It was very delicious! We had strawberries with it too. Me and Arthur had the biggest room and my dad was complaining because mum and dad had the smallest room.

My Lockdown Memories

James Bateman Class 2

During Lockdown, I got a new bike and learnt how to ride it without stabilisers.
I also remember coming out to the front of our house to clap for the NHS at 8pm every Thursday. My sister and me used to go out with pots and pans and bang about with our neighbours.
I remember having a huge VE day party where we painted our faces with the England flag and we were out all afternoon and evening celebrating with our neighbours.
We used to have many social distance gatherings with our neighbours on our own front gardens it was a lot of fun.
During the very hot days, my dad would get out the paddling pool and we would have a great time getting wet and having water fights all afternoon.
I remember my mum turning on the news to look for speeches and updates on the coronavirus news.
I remember feeling very bored as we were unable to go out to do anything.
I remember being very excited when my mum finally allowed

me to download Roblox and Minecraft over the summer.
On my sister's birthday in August, we hired a bouncy castle and had great fun.
I remember being jealous of my sister when I had to go back to school in June but she could still stay home. I remember doing lots of White Rose Maths and BBC Bitesize. I used to love playing all the little maths (and other) games on Bitesize once I finished my home learning.
I used to wake up early and get my work over and done with so that I could play for the rest of the day.

My Lockdown Memories

Grace Chorlton Class 2

When I was in lockdown:

I played badminton a lot. I went for lots of walks.
I liked playing maths games on the computer.
I had lots of work to do. I liked doing work because I could do it outside.
I liked making obstacle courses.
I liked going to Statham because we got an ice-cream.
I liked making jam tarts and cakes.
I liked lockdown but I didn't like not seeing my friends so I phoned them.

My Lockdown Memories

Evie Clair Class 2

I quite liked being in lockdown because it was fun.

My favourite part was being at my mum's school. I met loads of new friends but we couldn't touch each other. When we were there we did lots of fun work and we even had lunch there.

At home we played out lots and on sunny days we had the paddling pool out. We went on lots of walks to Spud Wood and I enjoyed it so much! I missed my friends so much so we kept in touch on 'Zoom' and it made me very happy. We made lots of rainbows and we even made a rainbow on our drive for the NHS.

It was so nice to be with my family and I will always remember it.

My Lockdown Memories

Lizzy Clemens Class 2

L oved spending time with my family
O nly allowed out for one hour
C lapping on the doorstep for the NHS
K eeping safe and washing my hands
D idn't get to see my friends
O llie my brother made me laugh
W e decorated our windows with rainbows
N ever missing face-time with my grandma
 and grandads

My Lockdown Memories

Elliot Cope Class 2

I played with Isaac on the Xbox - it was fun.
I played board games with my family and went on Zoom with my friends.
I played football and rugby with my Dad and brother.
I threw an American football with my brother and he winded me!
I enjoyed doing Oti Mabuse dance classes.
I hugged my cats a lot.

My Lockdown Memories

Sam Dilcock Class 2

I remember that I played video games.

On my birthday I got presents, one was a Star Wars game. I had a Pikachu cake, it tasted delicious. My Grandma came and we were in the garden. We had a special lunch with sandwiches and cakes. It was really yummy!

I really missed spending time with my family and friends, especially Lizzy. We were all a bit scared of the virus, but we stayed indoors to keep safe.

My Lockdown Memories

Freya Doyle Class 2

I played on the bouncy castle with my brother Jack. We went on long walks with my dog, who is called Rosie. I slept in a tent in the garden with Mummy and Jack. We made Welsh cakes and muffins, then we ate them. I played in the garden and the paddling pool. We played board games together. I spoke to my friends and family on Zoom.

My Lockdown Memory

Nella Dunkley Class 2

I went camping in my garden. We had little tents outside. My mum and dad went in one tent and I shared mine with my brother and my dog. Whilst my brother and my dad put up the tents me and my mum went for a walk with my dog Lili. When it was our bed time I was scared so my brother gave me a hug, then I was happy but I still couldn't get to sleep. I cuddled my dog Lili for a bit then I went to sleep.

My Lockdown Memories

Alex Gallagher Class 2

Water in the pond, catching frogs,
Happy to be with my mummy,
Everyone loves Gallagher Tree School!
Nothing was normal.

The trampoline was fun!
Home school was exciting,
Emma, Katie and Alex playing spies.

Orange pumpkin seeds in pots,
Running around the garden together,
Loving picnics on the grass.

Daddy and me played football,
Climbing on the fort with my sisters,
Learning maths outside,
Over the canal bridge, walking with Hoopy.

Snuggled together reading stories,
Everyone went on walks in the woods,
Don't want this time to end!

My Lockdown Memories

Lucia Giblin Class 2

I am going to tell you about my lockdown memories.
I went in the paddling pool and I had a barbecue and we did some planting in the garden. We planted some flowers and vegetables and fruits. Only the tomatoes survived. And my sunflower grew much bigger than my sister's!!
Every afternoon we would go on our bikes for miles. One day we took a picnic to a field and had our lunch there.
My Daddy still had to go to work on some days because he is a Plumber.
My sister had her birthday in lockdown. She had some friends round to sing happy birthday but they were not allowed to come inside.
We had a party for VE Day in our front garden, Mummy and Daddy put flags and paper lanterns all in the trees in our garden.

My Lockdown Memories

Freddie Gregory Class 2

I remember PE with Joe.

I also remember playing on my Nintendo Switch, which Daddy bought for me in lockdown.

During lockdown I also played lots of sports in the garden and at Sowbrook. I played football, rugby, cricket and croquet.

I went in the paddling pool a lot because the weather was hot and sunny.

My Nan and Grumps also sent us a badminton net through the post, so I played badminton with my family.

My sister and I played lots of games like Harry Potter and Danger Mouse.

Every day I went to walk my dog with my family. We went around the Dam and to Sowbrook.

I also did lots of fun baking. I made s'mores, scones and gingerbread men – yum!

Every day in the morning I did reading with my Nan and Grumps or my Grandma and Grandad over FaceTime. I also went on Zoom with my friends in the afternoons. We did quizzes and finding games and memory games over Zoom.

With my Auntie Dominique, I did FaceTime dancing and singing routines – it was really fun.
I remember learning about the history of Lymm and the creatures that live at the Dam during home schooling.
I had a nice time with my family during lockdown, but I really missed playing with my friends.

My Lockdown Memories

Poppy Harrison Class 2

Summer 2020 was so much fun!

We had just moved into our new house and then in March we didn't go to school for ages. Instead, we all stayed safe at home, away from the virus and helped the NHS.

It was lovely and warm, day after day of sunshine and we played and played in the garden. We got a new trampoline, played in the paddling pool, even on the slip and slide. I got a teepee and a swing set for my 6th Birthday and we stayed up late roasting marshmallows on our new firepit. I even had a zoom craft party with all of my friends!

We saw rockets launch live from America and saw their bright lights in space from our very own window.

When it rained we made dens, watched movies and had sleepovers in different rooms with my brothers. Grandma even facetimed me to read a bedtime story and I loved that so much.

We went on walks most days- explored our village and found new places that we never even knew existed, like Spud Wood and its amazing rope swings just 5 minutes from home!

We painted rainbows for the NHS and clapped on our doorstep with our new neighbours and on VE day we had an amazing afternoon tea delivered to our door by our friends at The Sanctuary Café.
We didn't need to go on holiday to another country, instead we went to Cornwall when we were allowed and it was the best summer ever.

My Lockdown Memories

Ellie Horner Class 2

I spent lots of time with my family and I did every single PE with Joe Wicks.

I read lots of different books to Granny over zoom.

Also, I went camping with relatives and my cousins and played on the beach.

We bought a new trampoline that was green and I had lots of fun bouncing on it.

I went on lots of walks and did lots of bike rides.

I went to Freya's and Evie's party at Freya's house, then it was Lulu's birthday so I had lots of cake.

Lulu got an allotment for her birthday and we enjoyed growing lots of fruits and vegetables.

I did lots of science experiments and my favourite one was bubbling witches brew.

In lockdown I missed my friends but I zoomed them so that we could stay in contact.

We made lots of cakes in lockdown including Lulu's birthday cake.

I did Poppy's and Eleanor's zoom parties.

My brothers and sister wrestled me all the time. I had lots of fun.

I loved lockdown.

My Lockdown Memories

Freya Inskip Class 2

When it was lockdown, I was missing all my friends. But I liked spending time with my family. Every day I had a really big walk or bike ride with all of my family, and we counted the rainbows in people's windows. One of our walks went by the canal where we skimmed rocks. One time I slipped into the canal and I got very wet and dirty! My mum said I was very brave because I went right under the water. My dad was working from home so he could eat tea with us every night which usually doesn't happen, and we got to eat outside most nights.

It was extremely hot during lockdown, I got very tanned! We got the paddling pool out a lot and we bought a sprinkler which was lots of fun too. It was my sister's birthday during lockdown, and she got a giant trampoline, and I went on it a lot and practiced flips. On really hot days we put the sprinkler under the trampoline, it sprayed up as we were bouncing which was excellent! We had a brilliant time making crazy golf courses and obstacle courses in our garden.

In lockdown we planted lots of different vegetables in

our garden. My favourite vegetable that we grew were the tomatoes and we also got a lot of mange tout. We have got a lot of pumpkins growing as well as courgettes. All the vegetables are really good.

We did clapping every Thursday night to thank the key workers that were working for us and trying hard to beat coronavirus. I saw my friend Poppy when we were clapping as she lives over the road so I could wave to her.

I was lucky that I got to go back to school before lots of other classes because that meant I got to see my friends.

There were some good parts of lockdown as I got to spend lots more time with my family and we had a lot of fun doing different things together in our house and garden, but I did miss my friends, nana, grandma and grandad and speaking on zoom was not the same as seeing them!

My Lockdown Memories

Anya James Class 2

The things that I missed the most during lockdown was playing games with my friends and going to the trampoline park. I kept in touch with some of my friends and family by doing video and telephone calls.

I went to my cousin's house and camped in their back garden, it was very exciting and we had lots of fun. In their garden was a big climbing frame. The climbing frame had swings, monkey bars, a slide and a trampoline. Playing on it was so much fun!

The next day when we came home it was sunny, so we got the paddling pool out in our garden and played lots of games. One of the games that I played was catch with my mummy, we managed to get all the way up to 170 without dropping the ball. If one of us dropped the ball we would have to go all of the way back to zero and start again. We also put our big tent up in the house and did some camping in our dining room.

On one of the sunny days I got some chalks out and drew some colourful bunting along the fence. I also did a beautiful rainbow picture that we hung in our living room window for everyone to see.

On Thursday evening I would stay up until 8pm so I could do a clap for the keyworkers, I used to take out a spoon and a pan and banged it as loud as I could.

I really enjoyed lockdown because I got to spend lots of time with my family and we did lots of exciting things together.

My Lockdown Memories

Katie Jolley Class 2

In lockdown we had my 6th birthday and I got a new bike.
We had Easter and I got lots of nice treats.
It was then my sister Lucy's birthday.
We had VE Day and a street party to celebrate and I made flags for outside and baked cakes to share.
We then had another street party to celebrate my Daddy's special birthday.
We did lots of walking and walked up Helsby Hill and spent days on the beach with our family.
I was happy in lockdown playing in my garden and spending time with our new Guinea pigs, Charm and Tiddles.

My Lockdown Memories

Aaron Kimmel Class 2

I'd like to share with you some of my favourite lockdown memories.

I went in my paddling pool in the garden on a very hot day but it got a hole in it.

I did lots of school work every day except for Saturday and Sunday.

My birthday was during lockdown. I didn't have a party or any friends over because it was in the middle of lockdown and we weren't allowed. I had coco pops for my breakfast and the house was full of balloons. There was lots of cake. I had a Zoom party with my friends and had lots of fun. I got a new mountain bike for my birthday which was fast and a Manchester United kit. It was a good birthday even though we couldn't go out anywhere.

We went out walking most days and had to keep social distance, we crossed the road whenever we saw people to keep out of their way.

I missed my friends during lockdown but we used Zoom to talk to each other. We played some games on our Zoom calls;

we had a treasure hunt and also a football quiz. I had a joke book and told lots of jokes to my friends.

I spoke to my grandparents on the telephone and read stories to them every night.

I played lots of football in the garden with my brother and bounced on our trampoline.

I liked lockdown, I had lots of fun.

My Lockdown Memories

Louis Kimmel Class 2

I'm going to tell you some of my favourite and interesting lockdown memories.

I played lots of football with dad in the garden and I scored lots of goals. I got really good at football during lockdown. Aaron and I took turns to go in goal and shoot.

Some of my favourite foods during lockdown were honey on toast, pancakes, pasta and roast dinners with Yorkshire puddings.

I spoke to my friends on Zoom. We played games and chatted. We had to make up our games which were fun. I liked the football quiz, treasure hunt and the guessing game.

I missed seeing my grandparents during lockdown but I used to ring them and read a story to them over the phone.

My birthday was during lockdown. It was different to other birthdays because I couldn't have any friends over or have a big party. Instead we had a big tea party with cakes and sandwiches and I Facetimed my friends.

Every Friday we watched the praise assembly with Mrs Graham. One week Aaron and I got a certificate. This made me feel very happy and excited, I liked seeing Mrs Graham.

I liked spending every day with my mum, dad, and brothers because I liked being at home with them and doing lots of maths.

When I was told lockdown was over and I was going back to school I felt shocked because only class F, class 1 and class 6 had to go back. It felt strange being back in school after all that time off but I liked seeing my friends and the teachers made us feel very happy to be back.

My Lockdown Memories

Aniyah Lamb Class 2

I went around Lymm dam and collected conkers.
I went to the dentist and they said I had a wobbly tooth.
I went on my space hopper.
I did colouring when I was bored.
I watched a film on my bunk bed.

My Lockdown Acrostic Poem

Charlotte Leach Class 2

L earning to ride my bike
O nly talking to my family on zoom
C lap for carers
K eeping people safe

D igging a veg patch
O nline Beavers sessions
W ishing I could see my friends
N ot going to school and learning at home
  with mummy and daddy

My Lockdown Memories

Phoebe Lilleywhite Class 2

I liked lockdown because I got to see my family a lot and I got to sleep in. I did not like lockdown because I did not get to see my friends. My Grandma got a new cat named Xanthe. I went on lots of walks around Lymm with my parents . I had a Bbq. I liked lockdown because I could just chill out and watch movies and popcorn and we did nothing.

My Lockdown Memories

Freya Loxham Class 2

I was happy and a bit sad. But I had fun spending time with my family.

We got a new paddling pool, I played in my paddling pool with my big sister Isla.

On one of our walks we found a big, high quarry in spud wood. The next day we went back and made a zip wire. It was lots of fun.

One day me and Isla decided to make a cinema in our living room, it was fun.

We missed McDonalds during lockdown so Mummy and Daddy made us a McDonalds drive through in my house.

We clapped for the carers outside our house. One night our Daddy came down the road on his bike whilst we were clapping it was funny. One night we use cooking pans and cooking spoons.

One night we camped outside in our garden. We didn't camp in a normal tent, we slept under a tarpaulin. It was fun. We cooked camping beans on a fire. They were delicious. In the morning we had breakfast then we went inside.

My Lockdown Memories

Eleanor Mayers Class 2

We went to the field and played chase with my little sister.

I made an obstacle course in my garden.

Sometimes I felt sad because I missed my friends and school.

I enjoyed doing lots of painting.

In lockdown I learnt to ride my scooter really fast!

My Lockdown Memories Acrostic Poem

Annabel O'Leary Class 2

L ockdown was sad but I had fun
O n Thursdays we banged pots and pans in
our dressing gowns, everyone else clapped
C oronavirus made us stay at home, I missed
my teacher and my friends
K ids did home school, my mummy and daddy
were terrible teachers!
D addy squirted water at me in the garden,
the weather was fun and hot
O n VE day we had a party outside and ate
delicious food
W e planted tomatoes, sweetcorn and
sunflowers in the garden
N ow I am happy I can go back to school and
see my friends
M y memory from lockdown is all about how
much fun I had
E veryone in my neighbourhood had lots of
fun!

M ummy looked after us everyday and made
me smile
O ur family did craft and painting
R unning with Joe Wicks was a good way to
start the day
I watched the pumpkin as it grew
E motions were worried and scared
S tay safe signs were in windows with rainbows

My Lockdown Memories

William Paramore Class 2

I did PE with Joe Wicks every day.

I liked lockdown a bit because I was able to go on a bike ride every day. I could play on my tablet. I also went to Freddie's house for the first time. I was very excited. It was so much fun. Freddie had monkey bars, swings and a slide.

In lockdown I learned how to make banana bread, scones and flapjacks. Now I can make them all by myself.

Every Thursday my family and I clapped for the NHS. It was at 8 o'clock so I was able to stay up until 8 o'clock on Thursdays.

I missed my friends very much. I missed my grandad in Ireland very much. I missed my 2 grandmas and my 2 grandads in England very much.

I couldn't do swimming or football or tennis or any type of sport.

I couldn't go to McColls every Friday to spend my pocket money.

I was very happy that I learned how to do the rainbow flick. I can now do a rainbow flick and a header and one time I did 9 keepy uppies.

On VE Day we had a party on our street and me and James were doing some skilful passing with his kicker ball on the road. We had a very good time.

My Lockdown Memories

Joshua Peers Class 2

I remember buying my bunk bed so I could share a room with my brother. It was fun because I spent time with my family. I did really miss my friend Alex so much though.

When we were at home, we made loads of cool superhero films. I splashed in the paddling pool lots with my brother Ben. We had to speak to our big family on Zoom. We played Guess Who together over the computer.

Later on, in the summer, I went camping with my friends. I also went to Paultons Park. My favourite ride was the Velociraptor. It went 40mph! It was amazing.

My Lockdown Memories

Edward Southworth Class 2

During lockdown I enjoyed spending more time with my Mummy. I helped Mummy to bake cakes but I did miss going to The Sanctuary Cafe in Lymm.
I did video calls with Josh, Charlotte and Louis and Aaron.
I remember clapping for the NHS.
I visited Lymm dam with my Mummy where I would ride my bike and I played in the field at Pluto Cottage with my Daddy. We made a den to keep us cool when the sun was shining and completely covered my legs with sand from the den!
I remember VE Day, it was to celebrate winning World War II. I remember my street had a party to celebrate. I think my Mummy and Daddy purchased an OSMO kit for me on the same day. I was very happy. During the street party I was dressed as a pirate and I was there with my Mummy and Nanna. The girls from my street put on a dance show which was very good!
I did miss school during lockdown but I wasn't unhappy.

My Lockdown Memories Poem

Henry Thomas Class 2

My lockdown memories all recorded in a book
For future generations one day to look.
Throwing beanbags, balls, scrunched up paper
in bowls and jugs.
Lots of time to practice my Makaton, hand
writing, drawing and to receive hugs.
'What's in the bag?' and counting blocks were
fun to play.
These are my memories from home schooling
with Mummy each day.

My Lockdown Memories

Isaac Watt Class 2

March 2020 was when the coronavirus came.
The coronavirus made us stay in our houses. This time was called lockdown.
During lockdown I went for bike rides and I went to Beavers through my computer.
Every Thursday we clapped the NHS and painted rainbows.
We also painted a Union Jack for 75 years after VE day.
I felt both happy and sad during lockdown.
I hope everyone learns a valuable lesson from this time.

My Lockdown Memory Box

Holly Antrobus Class 3

In my lockdown box I will put...
Schools closing because of Covid-19,
Doing live lessons on google classroom,
With my mum being the teacher.

In my lockdown box I will put...
Going out on a Thursday clapping for NHS at 8pm,
Drawing rainbows to stick on the windows
To say thank you.

In my lockdown box I will put...
Doing sports day at home
And PE with Joe Wicks,
Doing gardening in the back garden.

In my lockdown box I will put...
Face timing Poppy, Sophia and Eliza, to catch up,
Having a VE day street party,
Baking chocolate brownies for my family.

In my lockdown box I will put...

Getting more takeaways
And getting fish and chips,
Meeting up with Sophia to do dog walking.

My Lockdown Memory Box

Florence Barham Class 3

In my lockdown box I will put…
Schools shutting down because of Covid 19,
My mum being the teacher.

In my lockdown box I will put…
Clapping for heroes in my front garden at 8
pm,
Painting beautiful bright rainbows.

In my lockdown box I will put…
Schools opening for key worker children,
Doing online classes.

In my lockdown box I will put…
Having my birthday by zoom,
Going out for a walks and cycling my bike.

In my lockdown box I will put…
Doing more baking,
Some creative craft.

In my lockdown box I will put…
VE day, printing and colouring flags,

Having golden time at school.

In my lockdown box I will put…
Seeing my family on zoom,
Playing a lot of lovely games on my TV.

My Lockdown Memory Box

Luke Barnes Class 3

In my lockdown box I will put...
Schools shutting down because of Covid-19,
Doing lots of home schooling with my Mum,
Doing online lessons with my house group.

In my lockdown box I will put...
Cycling to Dunham Massey Ice Cream Farm,
Doing a 10K run with my Dad around Lymm,
Doing lots more walking than normal.

In my lockdown box I will put...
Playing socially distanced football with friends,
Doing lots of zooms with Rhys and Toby H,
In the park with friends at the end of term.

In my lockdown box I will put...
Camping in my bedroom with my sister,
Having more family movie nights,
Playing volleyball at Formby beach with family.

In my lockdown box I will put...
Playing cards against humanity family edition,

The Guinea pigs running on the trampoline,
Playing on the slip and slide with my sister.

My Lockdown Memory Box

Darcey Breeze Class 3

In my lockdown box I will put…
School shut down because of Covid 19,
Doing very easy online lessons,
My dad taught me at home.

In my lockdown box I will put…
Clapping for the NHS on my porch at 8pm,
Making a rainbow for NHS,
I love the NHS.

In my lockdown box I will put…
My aunt telling me that I can be a bridesmaid,
Missing my family and friends,
Getting more time on my ipad

In my lockdown box I will put…
My dogs birthday,
Making a big cake,
Going to the park and more bike rides,
Playing Monopoly on Saturday and Sunday.

My Lockdown Memory Box

James Burt Class 3

In my lockdown box I will put...
School shutting down because of Covid-19,
Going to Key Worker school.

In my lockdown box I will put...
Being in the park with my friends on my bike,
Cycling on the Trans Pennine Trail.

In my lockdown box I will put...
Painting rainbows for the NHS to say thank you,
Staying home to protect the NHS.

In my lockdown box I will put...
Walking next to the canal meeting Kate,
Going to Liverpool.

A Recipe for Lockdown

Cora Davies Class 3

Ingredients
A dollop of home-schooling
A handful of clapping for the NHS
A spoon of PE with Joe Wicks
A sprinkle of making a rainbow
A dollop of celebrating VE day
A blob of virtual beaver meetings
A swirl of celebrating birthdays
A spoon of key worker school
A hint of having family quizzes
A dollop of having family discos
A handful of helping at my new house
A drop of wearing a face mask

Instructions
First carefully put in a dollop of home-schooling.
Then happily chuck in a handful of clapping for the NHS.
After that independently throw in a sprinkle of making a rainbow.

Next energetically lunge in a spoon of PE with Joe Wicks.
Then slowly plunge in a dollop of celebrating VE (Victory in Europe) day.
After that quickly pour in a blob of virtual beaver meetings.
Then flip in a swirl of celebrating birthdays.
Next pour in a spoonful of key worker school and fry until golden brown.
After that pour in a hint of having virtual family quizzes.
Then drop in a dollop of having family discos.
Next put in a handful of helping at my new house.
Finally flip in a drop of wearing a face mask.

How to serve
Place the lockdown mixture into the world of lockdown madness.

My Lockdown Memory Box

Evie Dempsey Class 3

In my lockdown box I will put…
Schools shutting because of Covid-19,
Painting rainbows to go in my windows,
Practising doing gymnastics at home.

In my lockdown box I will put…
Doing home-schooling with my mum,
Seeing my friends on zoom,
Doing lessons online.

In my lockdown box I will put…
Doing more gardening and baking,
Having more exercise,
Enjoying more walking.

In my lockdown box I will put...
Getting a new trampoline,
Having more takeaways,
Going on bike rides with my brother.

In my lockdown box I will put…

Seeing my Nanny and Grandad through the window,
Chalking on the pavement,
Scooting down Booths Lane.

In my lockdown box I will put...
Drawing more pictures,
Having my birthday,
Doing crafts online,
Going to the park.

My Recipe for Lockdown

Toby Harrison Class 3

Ingredients
A sprinkle of PE with Joe Wicks
A cupful of missing football
A bit of clapping for NHS
A chunk of home schooling
A dollop of baking
A bit of drawing rainbows
A spoonful of family runs
A handful of family quizzes

Instructions:
First sprinkle a bit of PE with Joe Wicks carefully first thing in the morning .
Then quickly get a cup full of missing football and pour it in.
After that cut out a bit of clapping for NHS happily then throw it in.
Next find some home schooling independently and fry till it goes brown.
After that chuck in a dollop of baking roughly so the mixture

goes blondish.
Then put in some drawing rainbows quietly and put the mixture into a large bowl.
After that happily get some of the doing family runs and put a spoonful of it in the bowl.
Finally put in some family quizzes and stir it thoroughly.

My Lockdown Memories

Poppy Hopkin Class 3

In my lockdown box I will put...
Playing more games because we couldn't play with our friends,
Couldn't play on the zipline or the swings at the park.

In my lock down box I will put...
Home schooling because every school in the universe was shut down,
Having a picnic on VE day social distancing!

In my lockdown box I will put...
Having more movie nights than usual just for fun,
Doing lots of cycling on my purple bike,
Making bunting for Easter.

Lockdown Memories

Molly Howarth Class 3

In my lockdown box I will put...
School shutting down because of covid 19,
Being taught by dad and mum,
Doing lessons online in my PJs.

In my lockdown box I will put...
Clapping for the heroes at 8pm,
Making rainbows for NHS,
Facetiming friends from home.

In my lockdown box I will put...
Not seeing friends,
Washing hands more,
Playing football with my neighbours.

In my lockdown box I will put...
Quizzes with my cousin Chloe,
She did a Disney quiz,
I did an animal quiz.

In my lockdown box I will put...
Watching junior bake off,

Doing some baking,
Making new things.

In my lockdown box I will put…
Having movie nights,
Taking turns choosing the movie,
Having popcorn.

My Lockdown Recipe

Alexander James Class 3

Ingredients
A pinch of no schooling
A drop of home schooling
A sprinkle of Minecraft, Roblox and Fortnite
A cup full of clapping for NHS

Instructions
First add a pinch of no schooling.
Next add a drop of home schooling.
Then add a sprinkle of Minecraft, Roblox and Fortnite.
Now add a cup full of clapping for NHS.
After do some notebook art.
After that cook for 20 minutes.
Finally do some bike stunting.

My Memories of Lockdown

Evelyn Knowles Class 3

In my lockdown box I will put…
School shutting down because of Covid-19,
My mum and dad being my home schooling teachers,
Online lessons were very hard.

In my lockdown box I will put...
Missing my friends at school,
Meeting them on my google classroom,

In my lockdown box I will put…
Not going out,
Doing some baking,
Baking chocolate and banana muffins (they were very yummy).

In my lockdown box I will put…
Playing games with my sister,
Going for walks with my dog,
Visiting the beach (I liked it a lot).

In my lockdown box I will put...

A rainbow drawing for the NHS,
Clapping for the NHS at 8pm,
Watching lots of TV.

My Lockdown Memory Box

Sophie Lee Class 3

In my lockdown box I will put…
Schools shutting because of Covid-19,
Parents being teachers, everything changing,
Drawing rainbows and putting them in the window.

In my lockdown box I will put…
Every morning doing Joe Wicks,
Doing work for school,
Going for a bike ride on the Trans Pennine Trail,
Fun quizzes with family and friends.

In my lockdown box I will put…
Skype call with Poppy, Aimee and Eliza,
Playing in the garden with my sister,
Not going out to pubs,
Online lessons with my teacher at home.

My Lockdown Memory Box

Rhys Marrington Class 3

In my lockdown box I will put…
School shutting down because of Covid-19,
Homeschooling at my house,
Mum and Dad taking turns being the teacher,
Doing online lessons with my teacher.

In my lockdown box I will put…
Clapping for the NHS for all their hard work at 8pm,
Quizzes with my nan and grandad on Skype,
Playing family football in my garden,
Watching a movie some nights.

In my lockdown box I will put…
Camping in my bedroom for a week,
Playing in my garden more often with my sister,
Cycling round the dam with my family,
Getting really muddy and going to the ice cream van.

My Lockdown Memory Box

Jake McAfee Class 3

In my lockdown box I will put…
School shutting down because of coronavirus,
Having to homeschool,
Mum was the teacher for now.

In my lockdown box I will put…
Playing minecraft resort on my switch,
Playing on my trampoline with my sister,
Playing football.

In my lockdown box I will put...
Doing online lessons,
With my teacher Mrs Greason,
And chatting for a bit.

In my lockdown box I will put...
Playing on my Wii,
Going hiking and kayaking,
Doing lots of reading.

In my lockdown box I will put...
Doing a lot of bike rides,

Baking cakes,
Going horse riding.

In my lockdown box I will put...
Playing football,
Fun on the trampoline,
Tie-dyeing tops.

My Lockdown Recipe

Tofe Okoturo Class 3

Ingredients
Clapping for NHS
Wearing face masks
Spending time with my family
Joe Wicks
Online shopping
Painting rainbows

Instructions
First add a bit of clapping for the NHS into the bowl.
Pour the wearing face masks into the bowl and mix for 5 minutes.
Then rise the mixture for 10 minutes.
Next rest it.
Then add the gulp of spending time with family.
Then roll in Joe Wicks.
Put it in the oven for 40 minutes.
Use the online shopping to make icing
Take it out of the oven.

Decorate with painting rainbows.
ENJOY

How to serve
I am going to serve it to ME.

My Lockdown Memory Box

Aimee Paul Class 3

In my lockdown box I will put…
School shutting because of COVID-19,
Home schooling had to be done,
Being away from school was sad.

In my lockdown box I will put…
VE day social distancing street party,
A birthday treasure hunt which was marvelous,
So many skype calls with Sophie.

In my lockdown box I will put…
More movie nights,
Camping with my friends Memi and Ana,
Missing gymnastics and swimming.

My Lockdown Memory Box

Helena Pryers Class 3

In my lockdown box I will put...
School shutting because of Covid,
Homeschooling and mum being the teacher,
Doing fitness more often.

In my lockdown box I will put…
Clapping for the NHS on a Thursday night,
Putting up pictures of rainbows for key workers,
Staying at home to save lives.

In my lockdown box I will put…
Making my own classroom at home with mum,
Playing in the garden with my older brother,
Cycling down the Trans Pennine Trail.

In my lockdown box I will put…
Playing lots of tennis in the garden,
A load of DOG WALKS!
Having a garden party for my brother's birthday.

In my lockdown box I will put…
Learning new things,
Facetiming friends,
Going on adventures.

In my lockdown box I will put…
Bird watching (Blue Tips, Sparrows and Robins),
Reading about space,
Doing lots of painting.

My Lockdown Memory Box

Yuktha Ram Class 3

In my lockdown box I will put...
School shutting down because of Covid-19,
Home schooling,
My parents being the teachers.

In my lockdown box I will put...
Practising hula hooping,
Having presents for my birthday,
Baking if I am hungry.

In my lockdown box I will put...
Doing a lot more craft,
Playing with my dolls,
Watching more TV.

My Lockdown Memory Box

Toby Robinson Class 3

In my lockdown box I will put...
School shut down because of Covid,
Mummy and Daddy were the teachers,
Lessons online were very easy.

In my lockdown box I will put...
Missing my friends when I was at home,
Calling them on my mum's phone,
Not going outside so we stayed in the garden.

In my lockdown box I will put...
8pm on Thursdays clapping for NHS,
Painting rainbows to make people smile,
Making rainbows for our family.

In my lockdown box I will put...
Learning to make bread and cook tea,
Not going on holiday so we made a den,
Going on walks with my dog named Lottie.

My Lockdown Memory Box

Ella Sanderson Class 3

My lockdown box I will put...
School shutting because of the coronavirus,
Homeschooling with my sissy or mummy being the teacher,
Having private zoom calls with our house groups.

In my lockdown box I will put…
Doing lots of tik tok with my sisters and myself,
Playing robloxs a lot,
Playing on my xbox every day.

In my lockdown box I will put…
Watching old bake offs with my mummy, daddy and sissy,
Doing lots of walks,
Clapping for NHS at 8pm.

In my lockdown box I will put…
Having a VE day picnic,
Having a big BBQ with my family.

My Lockdown Memory Box

Kate Shaw Class 3

In my lockdown box I will put…
School closing and Mummy being the teacher,
Clapping for the NHS and key workers,
Missing my friends and family.

In my lockdown box I will put…
Camping in the garden with my brother and Daddy,
Key Worker school and homeschooling,
Putting up VE Day bunting in the window.

In my lockdown box I will put…
Doing weekly baking with my Daddy,
Not being able to shop with Mummy,
Going outside more to do exercise.

In my lockdown box I will put…
Playing with my brother more,
Having more time as a family,
Making plays and acting them out on video camera.

My Lockdown Memory Box

Reeva Sivagumaran Class 3

In my lockdown box I will put...
Schools shutting down the first time ever,
Homeschooling just because of Covid,
My mum was the teacher.

In my lockdown box I will put...
Mum starting her own 'leave no one behind' group,
Clapping for the NHS,
Making beautiful rainbows for my window.

In my lockdown box I will put...
Having my own family birthday just for me,
Playing games because I can't see my friends,
Talking on Lymm Radio.

In my lockdown box I will put...
Learning how to cycle,
Being very energetic,
Every Saturday walking to Lymm dam.

In my lockdown box I will put...

Looking at my old After School Club,
Playing badminton with my brother Rohan,
Downloading a new app called Seesaw.

My Lockdown Memory Box

Bonnie Taylor Class 3

In my lockdown box I will put…
School shutting because of covid-19,
Lessons online and my mum was my teacher,
The lessons online were hard.

In my lockdown box I will put…
Getting two new puppies called Mini and Candy,
Spending more time with my family,
Loving my friends but I couldn't see them.

In my lockdown box I will put…
NHS is my hero, I love NHS,
Clapping for the NHS at 8pm,
Painting a rainbow on my window.

In my lockdown box I will put…
Going on more bike rides with my daddy and his dog Teddy,
Walking more with Teddy and my dad,
Playing all day on my trampoline.

My Memory Box

Lisa Thornton Class 3

In my lockdown box I will put…
School was shut because of coronavirus,
Home schooling with my mummy and daddy,
Mum helped me with online schooling.

In my lockdown box I will put…
Clapping for NHS on Thursday,
My sister and I made a rainbow.

In my lockdown box I will put…
Playing on the road for VE day,
Making crumble with daddy.

In my lockdown box I will put…
When we went on a bike ride,
Going to the co-op on my scooter.

In my lockdown box I will put…
Going on my ipad,
We went on the switch ,
I went on my computer.

My Lockdown Memory Box

Lucas Thorpe Class 3

In my lockdown box I will put…
School locked down because Covid 19,
My mum and dad became teachers at home,
Doing easy lessons online.

In my lockdown box I will put…
Thursdays at home clapping at 8pm for NHS,
Sleepovers at home in my comfy room,
Playing games like battleships.

In my lockdown box I will put…
Going on google classroom to meet my friends,
Getting the Ipad at half past 4 to play Minecraft,
Playing games called Multicraft and Blockcraft,
Getting a new cat in lockdown called Max.

In my lockdown box I will put…
Doing lots of things as a family,
Camping out in the living room,
Growing our own lettuce and tomatoes.

In my lockdown box I will put…
Me and my mum making a chocolate cake,
Going on my bike with my mum and dad,
Holidaying in France, going by plane.

My Lockdown Memory Box

Eliza Walton Class 3

In my lockdown box I will put…
School closing for the first time because of coronavirus,
Doing sports day at home and my house group winning,
Learning from home with my mum teaching,
Coming down at 9.00 to check seesaw.

In my lockdown box I will put…
Clapping for carers on a Thursday at 8.00pm,
Going down in my pyjamas,
Fireworks blasting off.

In my lockdown box I will put…
Camping in the cold garden and toasting marshmallows,
With Benjy who normally gives me an occasional kick,
Camping in the garden for Benjy's scouts.

In my lockdown box I will put…
Going on lots of family evening bike rides,
Walking along the Trans Pennine Trail,
Biking with my mum and Benjy while they run,

In the mornings on Tuesdays and Fridays,
Doing a walk with my dad sometimes.

In my lockdown box I will put…
Baking crumbles and scones,
Baking cakes for my nanny,
Doing delicious puddings,
That smell so fantastic from the oven!

In my lockdown box I will put…
Doing Skype and Zoom with Aimee, Holly and Sophie,
Seeing Aimee doing brilliant flips on her bar,
Doing Zoom with my piano teacher.

In my lockdown box I will put…
Having my birthday with no one coming,
Having an exquisite seventh birthday cake,
Getting a disco light for my birthday,
Having a disco in the evening on my birthday.

In my lockdown box I will put…
Having discos,
Discos on Saturdays and Sundays,
Discos with sweet treats while dancing.

My Lockdown Memory Box

Poppy Wee Class 3

In my lockdown box I will put…
School shutting down because of Covid-19,
Home schooling with my parents in the morning,
Having zoom calls online with my teacher.

In my lockdown box I will put...
8pm Thursday nights clapping for NHS,
Painting beautiful rainbows to say thank you,
Staying home staying safe.

In my lockdown box I will put…
Skype calls with Sophie, Holly,
Zoom calls with Sophie, Eliza, Holly, Poppy H,
Facetime calls with my family.

In my lockdown box I will put…
Bike riding down the Trans Pennine Trail,
PE with Joe Wicks and my Dad,
Sports day in my garden.

In my lockdown box I will put…

Movie nights watching Jumanji with my family,
Playing Mario Kart for the first time with my sister.

My Lockdown Memory Box

Oscar Wilkinson Class 3

In my lockdown box I will put…
Schools shutting down because of Covid-19,
Home schooling with my mum,
Having sports day at home with my mum.

In my lockdown box I will put…
Painting rainbows as a thank you for the NHS,
Clapping on Thursday at 8pm,
Staying home, staying safe and saving lives.

In my lockdown box I will put…
Celebrating my sister's birthday,
Also celebrating Easter with my family,
Finally celebrating VE day.

In my lockdown box I will put…
Going on an eight kilometre walk,
Exercising more,
Playing outside in the garden a lot more.

In my lockdown box I will put…

Winning a Guinness World Record,
For doing an online drawing lesson,
Drawing lots more,
Having lots more fun.

In my lockdown box I will put…
Building a hedgehog house,
Me and my dad building it,
It's very colourful.

My Lockdown Memory Box

Sophia Wright Class 3

In my lockdown box I will put...
Schools shutting down because of Covid 19,
Starting home schooling with parents as teachers,
Having online lessons with your proper teachers.

In my lockdown box I will put...
Clapping for the NHS on Thursday nights at 8pm,
Painting rainbows for the NHS to go in our windows,
Celebrating the NHS on VE day.

In my lockdown box I will put...
Not being able to see my friends,
Zoom calls with Holly, Poppy W and Poppy H,
Having to social distance from my friends.

In my lockdown box I will put...
Coming down on my birthday,
Seeing presents piled on the sofa,
Opening presents with excitement,
Getting a happy feeling with my new things.

In my lockdown box I will put…
Doing extra baking,
Making different things,
Tasting delicious new things.

My Lockdown Memories

Arthur Agamian Class 4

Lockdown is what it is, as we live bit by bit,
We look back on the good,
Then we know we can get through it.

But the family times were quite good,
We kept our heads up high,
Then lockdown started to fly far, far away.

We stayed in touch and kept the love,
Though we couldn't hug,
We all got through it.

Then the world started to change,
So we played a funny game,
That seemed to be our new life.

We knew the masks and the handwash,
Were just to keep us safe but,
Something about this new life was not right!

Eventually we got used to it,
Though it was hard staying indoors,
But at least we still had each other.

When we hear that school is nearly back,
It lifts all our spirits,
Then we know our lives are coming back.

We started seeing friends and family more,
Which was another sign that our life,
Was returning, slowly but surely!

Diary of My Lockdown

James Anderson Class 4

I went fishing with Ollie and my Dad. We caught a lot of small tiny fish. It was a lot of fun and a guy next to us caught a really big fish. A man showed us how to put the maggots on the hook. It was a bit gross I really didn't want to do it but I did. When we caught the tiny fish they were very wriggly.

I played lots of Monopoly with my family. The games lasted very long. I liked the burger the most, Ollie liked the Race Car the most. My mum liked the Roller Skates the most and my dad liked the Plane the most. I got a 10 million pound hotel every round and obliterated them, but one round Ollie beat me. Only because he bought a 20 Million pound hotel and I became angry and stopped playing.

The very best thing I did in lockdown with my dad was make a JAMES DO NOT ENTER sign. I cut it out of wood with a power saw called a jig-saw. It took a few days to do it and required a lot of patience and at the end we spray painted it. It looked like space after we spray painted it. It looked COOL.

My dad and my brother made lots of bread together. It took a lot of kneading and effort to do. This was important to get air in the bread and while the bread was getting air, we went out on our bikes to the locks. When we got back it was enormous and we were amazed. After it went in the oven it tasted great and we put Nutella on. It was BRILLIANT.

My Lockdown Memories

Freya Antonelli Class 4

Lockdown was an experience of life,

Lockdown was sad because I missed my friends,

Lockdown was good because I got to spend more time with my family including my dog Monty,

Lockdown was brilliant because I got more time to practice art,

Lockdown was fun because I wrote a song with the help of a professional musician on Facetime and it was called Lockdown and it was about my feelings of lockdown,

Lockdown was amazing because I played on my Nintendo with my cousins more often,

Lockdown was fabulous because I got the time to go on 11 mile bike rides,

Lockdown was an excellent experience.

My Lockdown Experience

Lauren Caton Class 4

In my small village hometown,
We all sadly had to go into lockdown.
This experience was very unique,
As it went on week after week.
I did not get to see my friends or go to school,
Which was definitely not very cool.
We started learning in a different way,
Homeschooling started each and every day.
My Mum struggled with the maths,
And sometimes went down the wrong paths.
Despite all of this we had loads of fun,
BECAUSE....
I learnt to play cards,
And realised that I do not like jam tarts.
Reading Harry Potter filled my time,
And my science experiments included slime.
We rode our bikes for miles and miles,
And created lots of arts and craft piles.
Lego creations were in every room,

And we saw many friends and family on zoom.
We spent hours and hours on spud wood swings,
And did many, hazardous action things.
Learning paddle boarding and canoeing,
Were some of the many things I was doing.
Formby beach was a regular evening favourite trip,
Lots of fun bum boarding, sand dune jumping and the occasional chip.
One of the highlights was a trip to Aberdeen,
To visit cousins we had not seen.
I am FINALLY allowed back at Cherry Tree,
And from my parents I am free.
I am so glad to be back at school!

My Lockdown Memories

Felicity Corlett Class 4

In lockdown I made cotton candy with my family and I practised guitar. When it was lockdown I got new stuff to play with outside and me and my siblings got milkshakes. In lockdown, I have been doing a lot of reading and I have been doing colouring in my colouring book. When I was in home prison I went with my family on an isolated holiday to Pembrokeshire in Wales, it was called Heatherton World of Activities. In home prison, I got my two dogs, new toys and they really liked them. Still in home prison, I have been watching many movies and my Grandma and my Mum put plants, a gnome and a bird bed in my garden. On my isolated holiday my Dad got so sun-burnt he looked like a crab. Still on my isolated holiday, me and my family went to the beach and I found a rock that I called Billy Bob Bob. When I was still on my isolated holiday, I went to an activity centre and went on a big zip wire and played a lot of games. Still on the isolated holiday, me and my family went to the zoo! We saw a bunch of animals but there was so much walking! I went on a dragon slide and I nearly bashed my leg on the side of the slide and it was really fast! I went in the batting cage to play baseball and the machine was throwing the baseballs at me and I was really good at it. Still on this fun holiday, I went on a race car and I crashed it, but I was fine and I went on these really bouncy things that looked like pillows. That's why they're called jumping pillows. I went home and I played Hide and Seek with my brother and my sister but Will, my other brother, didn't play, because he was in his room on his phone.

Lockdown

Anna Davies Class 4

Dear Diary,

As soon as I woke up this morning, the bright, yellow sun beamed through my curtains and into my eyes. It was time to get up! As I went downstairs I thought to myself that it might be a good day to have the paddling pool out. I ran into the lounge and I asked my Mum. She said, "You can but you will have to blow it up first!"
"Oh!" I said. Louisa, Joe and I blew it up and filled it with clear, glistening water and then splashed in it all morning. It was SO MUCH FUN!

After that it was lunch time and we had a barbeque! That's my favourite! Whilst my dad was doing the barbeque, I played Yahtzee with the rest of my family and had a great time! When we had finished eating we all snuggled up and watched a film and of course we had some popcorn! It was really good! As soon as the film stopped, my Dad announced, "I think we need to get out of the house!"

"We could go on a bike ride!" I said excitedly. We grabbed our bikes and headed off on our usual route - The Trans Pennine Trail. When we got home and opened the door Paddy the dog ran as fast as he could to get to us but the hall door was shut. I opened it and Paddy jumped up to me and licked my face and then he did it to everyone else too. We all went to the garden and sat down, Louisa got everyone a homemade ice lolly - they were yummy! After we had finished our ice lollies Louisa, Joe, Mum and I went to the shops and got some dinner.

My dad had to stay at home and keep Paddy company, he also had to do some work. When we got back with the dinner, Mum said, "Are you hungry now?" I answered, "Yes I'm starving" so she put the dinner in the oven and waited for it to cook. Once it had cooked she served it and called everyone. We all ran into the kitchen, sat down and started eating greedily. We all finished at the same time! We must have been starving!

Me and Mum made an apple crumble in the morning so we put that in the oven and we all had that for pudding. It was bedtime after that so Joe, Louisa and I went upstairs and brushed our teeth. We had a story by Dad and we went to bed. I couldn't wait for the next day of lockdown!

My Lockdown Memories RAP!

Archie Deering-Short Class 4

In lockdown lots changed,
We had to mix it up and rearrange!
Not all was good not all was bad,
Staying at home was pretty rad!!!
The NHS were working so hard,
So we drew a big rainbow on a big, big card.
I got fit but missed McDonald's,
Had to play video games to drown
my sorrows!
I missed my friends, I missed my school,
Mum"s homeschooling was really NOT cool!!!
Social distancing not the best,
Wearing a mask is really a pest!!!
We baked some cakes and went to the beach,
The teachers zoomed so they could teach.
The weather was good the weather was bad
    but I didn't really care,
Because I had good news to share (my baby
    brother).

Lockdown was good, lockdown was bad,
But I tried really hard to not feel sad.
But most of all,
I LOVED being with mum and dad!!!

My Lockdown Memories!

Mimi Denton Class 4

At the beginning of the year we got a puppy and we called him Oreo! We were very excited to plan holidays with him but then came in...LOCKDOWN! Mother's day was our last 'free' day.

After that we were stuck at home and we could only go out for walks. We found lots of new places to walk around our house. We walked alongside the Manchester Ship Canal all the way to Thelwall, sometimes we went to Sowbrook which is a big field and on one of those walks we found a baby squirrel! We took the metal detectors and found some cool stuff too.

Home schooling was hard but sometimes it was fun because we got to do obstacle courses for our PE and we also did Joe Wicks every day! I did some online calls with my friends and one time we did an online craft session and a game of bingo.

The weather was really good throughout lockdown and we spent lots of time in the garden. We had the slip and slide out and we had lots of fun on it. We also had the pool out and we had a Nerf gun fight! Me and my mum painted some rocks and when the weather was rubbish we did some baking with my brother.

During summer we got a trampoline and I can do lots of tricks like back-flips, front- flips and lots more. I really enjoyed lockdown with my family but sometimes I didn't like it because I couldn't see my friends.

My Lockdown Memories

Isaac Finnnan Class 4

L ots of time in the garden, planting fruit and
flowers
O ften speaking with friends and family on the
phone
C leaning my bedroom and helping out around
the house
K eeping the oven on with baking
D og walks with my dog in the sun
O n most weekends I visited my dad in
Liverpool
W e went to Wales camping and caravanning
N ext to our apple tree we have built a pond

My Lockdown Memories

Katie Gallagher Class 4

Gallagher Tree School opened in my dining
room,
All three of us played outside at breaktime,
Love this school!
Lots of work to do,
And loads of fun.

Gardening and planting seeds,
Hope everyone in the world will be ok,
Eating picnics near the pond,
Radical because everything was closed.

Toss a ball for my dog Hoopy,
Rainbows for the NHS make me happy,
Every window looks colourful,
Everybody stays at home.

Some brave people kept us safe,
Chocolate cake to celebrate my birthday!
Hot walks in the fields,
Often we bounced on the trampoline,

Outside I played on the swings,
Loving lockdown - I'll never forget it!

My Lockdown Memories

Ben Gowland Class 4

L oved annoying my sister Bea
O ften we had film night with popcorn
C ouldn't stop wanting to see Seb
K eeping away from other people
D idn't like being home schooled
O range sun flowers growing in our front
    garden
W ooden raised bed made by us
N obody could come to play

My Lockdown Memories

Jessica Howcroft Class 4

My lockdown was quite boring to be honest, but we met a LOT of new people on our road that we never realised lived there.

We also discovered this place called Spud Wood. Spud Wood is a place you can walk dogs and there are rope swings which are really fun.

I really enjoyed it, when every other Friday, me and my family would have a movie night, and every other Friday we would have a games night. I also enjoyed when me and my family would sit at the table, because normally we eat at different times and we eat in the living room.

One of my favourite memories is when it was my little sister's first birthday. We didn't have a big party though because we were in lockdown, but we delivered birthday cake to some of the people who live on our road.

One of my other favourite memories is when I first saw my friends when we were allowed to meet with a maximum of six people.

In lockdown I also discovered this game called Roblox

which is a video game for kids. I spent quite a bit of time on the phone to my friends when I couldn't see them.

My least favourite memory is when my ginger cat died. Her name was Jingles. We got her before I was born so I had never been without her so that really ruined my lockdown. Sometimes I still cry about it.

We also went on a lot of bike rides and we would normally cycle to Spud Wood and then I would go on the ramps (I fell off quite a lot). We also went on a long walk every day down to this place called Wet Gate Lane and sometimes we would do a big loop all the way back to our house.

P.S I was VERY glad to be back at school.

My Lockdown Memories

Oliver Jack Class 4

When lockdown started I was happy to be at home with my family all of the time. I had lots of time to play my games.

The weather during the lockdown was very hot and sunny. We grew some carrots, strawberries, broccoli, onions and other vegetables so we didn't need to go out to the shops as much to buy food.

We weren't allowed to go on a summer holiday, so instead we went to the beach and slept in a caravan, but I hated it because I got sand in my shorts. We also went to visit Nanny and Grandad in Wales in our caravan. That was fun because I got to play with my remote control car.

I am happy to be back at school because I am enjoying maths in year 4 and playing with my friends too.

My Lockdown Acrostic Poem

Elsie Jagger Class 4

L ovely time with my amazing family
O utside sliding on my slip 'n' slide
C lapping for the NHS and carers
K nowing that I couldn't see my Dad made me
sad
D reaming that I could see my friends
O rdering Pizza Hut for tea because we
couldn't go to the pub
W orrying about Covid 19
N ew exercises with Joe Wicks!

Lockdown Memories

Joseph Kimmel Class 4

Dear Diary,

It's day five in lockdown. Everything is fun at home. I've been out on my skates today. I went superfast down a huge hill which was great. I'm missing my friends but not missing school work.

Dear Diary,

It's day ten in lockdown and unfortunately I am having to complete my school work every day. Fortunately, I can now see my friends on Zoom so that's good. I'm only allowed my electronics when I've finished my work in the afternoons. Today me and my brothers came up with a really good game called, "The Five Lives Game".

Dear Diary,

It's day twenty in lockdown. I'm really annoyed at the neighbours as today they keep shouting at us when we are playing in the garden. It's making me feel really sad that we can't have fun in the garden without them shouting at us. Things are tough enough as it is.

Dear Diary,

It's day thirty in lockdown. Today has been the best day, I met up with one of my friends and took their dogs for a walk. We climbed trees and went in lots of muddy water in our wellies. I got stuck in the mud and we laughed a lot.

My Lockdown Memories

Krzysztof Kraska Class 4

I remember during lockdown when we went to my cousin's house. When we got there I was so happy that I got to see him because I barely ever see him. We played video games and went in the pool. The pool was really fun because we acted like dolphins and fish.

I remember when I went to the park because it's probably the BEST park I've EVER been to. One time at the park, my dad was swinging me on the swing then I jumped off it. Next I went on a slide as big as an elephant and I went down it. It was so fast I almost fell off! When I got down I had NO IDEA what just happened.

I also remember the time I went to a restaurant for my birthday. It was so fun because we got to design masks that look like glasses. We got to play Noughts and Crosses and I played against my sister. It was SO FUN!

My Lockdown Memories Acrostic Poem

Temi Okoturo Class 4

L ovely time with my family
O dd places to walk
C olouring rainbows to stick on the windows
K icking about a ball in the garden
D oing some baking at home
O ut in the park
W alking with my friends and family
N ice time at home

Dear Mum

Benjamin Paramore Class 4

Dear Mum,

I am looking though some photos and they are really reminding me of our lockdown story. I wanted to write you a letter about it.

At the end of March our school closed and we had to stay in our house. I couldn't see my friends and I couldn't do any sports like football, tennis or swimming.

We had to wash our hands lots, every time we came in. We also had to use hand sanitisers. I'm not a fan of sanitiser because it burnt my hand. This made me sad because I love seeing my friends and playing football. The photos are reminding me of all the memories that I enjoyed like make rainbow pictures for our window, going for walks, climbing trees, running and practising keepy upies.

Then it was Easter and we did lots of eggcellent drawing and crafts. I was really pleased to win a drawing competition at your work. Do you remember the jigsaw we made? It took us two days to complete it.

Mum I've worked out how many times we sang Happy Birthday during lock down. It's eleven (that's not even including my friends that had birthdays during lockdown). I've lost count of how many bike rides we did. We did lots of art and painting, we drew a poster about Earth Day but my favourite piece of artwork was the ice cream pinata that we made. Could you guess how many ice creams we had? I reckon about fifty ice creams!!!

It was great that the sun was shining which meant that William and I played in the paddling pool, grew monster sunflowers, explored new fields and you made us a tent that we could put up in the garden. Every single one of these things made me feel happy. Did these things make you happy too? I bet you love all the apple and rhubarb pie I made. I was an expert at the lattice for the pie. It was a delicious pie.

Every Thursday night we used to go and clap for the NHS. You and dad clapped your hands and William and I used a wooden spoon to hit against a saucepan to make as much noise as we could. I hit it so hard and I accidentally broke the wooden spoon.

I hope you enjoyed my lockdown memories.

In The Year 2020

Vivek Rao Class 4

Year 2020 we will never forget,
Covid-19 struck and we had to stop the
spread,
People getting sick and dying everyday,
So lockdown came to keep Covid at bay.

Year 2020 we will never forget,
Using hand sanitiser and face masks to
protect,
Fun activities cancelled and banned,
Birthday parties not going as planned.

Year 2020 we will never forget,
Homeschooling with Google Classroom was
set,
To keep the nation healthy with an exercise
fix,
We kept fit daily with Joe Wicks.

Year 2020 we will never forget,
Queuing in the rain to buy a playset,

Clapping on Thursdays for all those doing their
best,
And painting rainbows for the NHS.

Year 2020 we will never forget,
Enjoying family Zoom calls over the internet,
Schools reopening Covid-secure,
Delighted to see friends again as before.

In the year 2020 Covid-19 came,
History will say,
It will never be forgotten,
Forever and a day.

My Lockdown Memories

Imogen Roberts Class 4

What I did in Lockdown is that I did my homework from class three because I hadn't moved up to Class 4 yet. After I did my homework I played on my XBox. Then I would watch Netflix for an hour.

During the holidays it was my birthday. On my birthday I got lots of presents such as a keyboard and mouse for my computer, XBox vouchers, a Roblox gift voucher and I had a small party with my cousin. It was great and I got to go to TGI Fridays and eat lots of birthday cake!

Later that night, I thought of my Great Great Granddad when a rainbow appeared in the sky and that made me feel happy.

My Lockdown Memories

Seren Roberts Class 4

During my lockdown I did lots of art such as bunting for the VE day and drawing rainbows to support the NHS. Also, every Thursday we clapped to the NHS for their very hard work and for saving lives, they are superheroes.

We were keeping fit doing different sports like PE with Joe Wicks, yoga, meditation and Brenda's boot camp.

Our neighbour made quizzes to keep people happy and gave us a new one every week.

We celebrated and made parties at home like Easter and even my birthday!.

My Lockdown Memories

Sophie Sharples Class 4

I enjoyed spending time with my family. We went out for walks and found new paths to explore. I also enjoyed playing with my toys.

I missed seeing my friends and going to school but I was able to see them on google classroom. I was sad that I couldn't go to swimming, Brownies and gymnastics. Also, running club and clay creators.

There were plenty of activities that kept me busy. I loved painting rocks with all different designs for my cousins, friends and grandparents. I helped plant some fruit and vegetables in the garden and water them.There was plenty of room for me to pogo, rollerblade, cycle and scoot around the garden. It was so much fun!

I kept in touch with my family and friends on facetime and zoom. It was nice to see them but very weird that we could only see them on a screen.

I made some rainbows with lego, paint, chalks and colouring pencils. I loved creating them and it was fun spotting them in windows on our walks. There were big ones, small ones and some were made out of sticks and pine cones.

Each week we clapped for key workers, carers and NHS. There were lots of people out and it was very loud.

My Lockdown Diary

Sullivan Stewart Class 4

Dear Diary,

In lockdown things have been different, like us not being able to visit our friends but I have still been calling them a lot! Every day of lockdown, scientists have been working hard to help stop Covid-19, all day and all night!

The day before Legoland closed we went to sleep there! No one was there so we got it all to ourselves! It was great and my mum was nearly sick on the spinning ride!

In the middle of August my parents bought a new house, now my mum lives in the new house and my dad stays in the other one and we switch between them. Lockdown also gave me the great opportunity to read all seven Harry Potter books, they were great!!!

Every day of lockdown we did Joe Wicks and my dad joined in every session (a show on YouTube, guess who it was run by?) Monday-Friday 9am-9:30am! It really was fun and we did it every morning! Every Friday he had a dress up exercise session which was epic!!!

See! We weren't able to go on holiday in lockdown even though it was the summer holidays but we still had lots and lots and lots of FUN!!!!

Sometimes my mum would make delicious homemade pizzas! We would also get to put on the toppings of our pizza, every day we asked for them but only got them on Fridays.

Every day mum, me and my sister went out on bike rides down the Trans Pennine, my mum got this one wheeled bike that clips on to the back of hers and I got a new bike that looks epic. It's a red one!

Lockdown Memories

Hannah Swettenham Class 4

L ovely memories of lockdown were made,
sharing time as a family, painting rainbows,
playing games and watching films

O n my birthday I had a lovely time with a few
friends outside in the garden, eating cake
and party food

C lubs are different, I wish I could go to
gymnastics, swimming and Brownies

K eeping fit with my family doing Joe Wicks,
cycling and walking

D igging in the garden, planting carrots, beans,
peas and flowers

O n VE day, we celebrated with bunting and
had a tea party in the street

W ater play in the garden and bouncing on the
trampoline in the sun

N ice time baking, eating yummy flapjacks,
brownies and cakes

My Lockdown

Summer-Bleu Taylor Class 4

In lockdown we went on lots of bike rides,
In lockdown we walked the dogs,
In lockdown I learnt how to do a back flip,
In lockdown we got two new dogs,
In lockdown I learnt how to do a front flip,
In lockdown we got a new hot tub,
In lockdown we went on lots more walks,
In lockdown I got a new hover cart.

My Lockdown Memories

Layla Thoma Class 4

The 23rd of March was a very strange day as it was the first day of lockdown and also my brother's 12th birthday. It seemed so strange to wake up on a Monday morning to realise that I didn't have to go to school that day, or the day after that! It was so nice to spend quality time with my family, even my Stepdad was home for two weeks! Each day that went by we walked and walked and enjoyed the beautiful sunshine.

I learnt how to complete my schoolwork and lessons online, at first I thought that this would be impossible but after some time I got used to it and it became the new normal. The Easter holidays passed and I was very sad as I couldn't fly to see my family in Cyprus but then in June I was told I could travel, so I did, I was so happy when I saw my family.

In August I came home from Cyprus, after 2 lovely months and I was so happy to be back home again. I was so excited to go back to school to see all my friends and join my new class. The thing I missed the most during lockdown was my school.

My Lockdown Memories

Caitlin Thomas-Berry Class 4

I loved going on bike rides and having long walks with my family.
I had my 8th birthday in lockdown and we had a hot tub and gazebo, so we could enjoy the hot tub even in the rain.
I loved spending time with my family.
I also loved spending time with my dogs and Face-timing friends.
It was so much fun when I got my trampoline and when it was put up I used it straight away.
It was difficult when we had to do home school because I missed school and my friends.
When lockdown was eased we went up to my caravan and had long walks on the beach and played games.

Lockdown Memories

Eddie Walker Class 4

L ovely memories
O kay days
C lapping for carers
K illing the coronavirus
D own days
O ften washing hands
W alking dogs
N ot touching people

Lockdown Memories

Charlie Watson Class 4

L ocked up in our house
O n my laptop alone
C oronavirus spreading
K eep washing my hands
D ad getting poorly
O k now he's better
W earing face masks in summer
N ow finally back to school

My Lockdown Memories

Tom Williams Class 4

I enjoyed being at home during lockdown.

I enjoyed playing computer games, on my own and online with my friends.

I stood with my mummy every week to clap for carers. I used to wave to our neighbours when we did this!

We didn't do the Joe Wicks workout - we did our own boot camp workout in the garden every afternoon when we had finished the home school work. Sometimes our dog would join in too!

I played Chess, Monopoly and The Game of Life. My favourite was Monopoly because I used to win a lot!

I would walk my dog with my mummy after lunch and she would point out all the rainbow drawings in the windows of the houses.

I missed seeing my grandparents. I would Zoom with my best friend and we would play 1 computer game together. I chose

2 masks, one with robots on and one with sharks on.

My Lockdown Memories

Dexter Williamson Shields Class 4

During lockdown, I enjoyed building LEGO with my Dad. My dog was always jumping on my bed with me.

In the week, me and my Mum and the dog walked around the block. Me and Hannah baked brownies, lemon drizzle cake and fruit bars. I also played on my PS4. I especially enjoyed playing Fall Guys, Fortnite and Steep.

My Lockdown Memories

Emily Zverblis Class 4

Things I enjoyed

I enjoyed home learning because my Mummy was a good teacher in Lockdown and I loved the playtime with Mabel. Every time we did Joe Wicks, Mabel tried to join in and play ball and she was funny. I had my very own vegetable patch and we grew tomatoes, carrots, sugar snap peas and beetroot.

It was so sunny I played in the paddling pool with Mabel but she didn't like it. We walked to the park to collect sticks to build a big den in my garden.

We went to pick blackberries on our bikes and I had fun doing sports day in the garden.

We clapped for the NHS with pans and with wooden spoons

.

Me and my mum painted rainbows together and put them in the window.

Things I missed

I missed all my friends and teachers because I wasn't allowed to see them. I missed my cousins and Nanna and Granddad and we did a family zoom every Thursday. My cousin had a good zoom birthday party and we sang happy birthday and they blew out the candles on the cake I did a zoom with Sophie everyday .

Special Days

At Easter me and Mabel did an Easter egg hunt together in the garden and Mabel did it but with dog treats.

Lockdown Memories

Katie Allan Class 5

I Remember…
Me, my brother and my little sister were playing in the paddling pool, we were jumping from the trampoline into the pool. One time I was jumping and my brother pushed me and I fell head first. Then my brother started to laugh. After that we started to jump from the chair. After we started to jump from the chair it was time to get revenge. As my brother was jumping I poured ice water on him. He was so mad!

I remember…
Me, my brother, my little sister and my mum loved baking in Lockdown. we mostly baked cakes but we also liked baking cookies like ginger ones and chocolate cookies and my little sister flicked melted chocolate in my face. I was so mad but I decided not to get revenge. But I decided to prank her with water balloons lucky my brother had just bought some so I grabbed some and filled them up. After I had filled some up I brought her outside and said it was a magic trick then I threw them at her after that I thinks she hates me!

Lockdown Memories

Zoe Archibald Class 5

Home and school

I remember lockdown was really hard because my mum and dad were not proper teachers. Dad would help me sometimes and my mum would help me sometimes. I was very angry because I could not see my friends. Sometimes we were at school which was much better than at home. At school we had to be in bubbles. I think lockdown has somethings.

NHS

During lockdown the NHS has been saving people's lives. People over 11 have been wearing face masks to keep safe. You have to keep 2 meters apart from each other to keep safe. The coronavirus has killed millions of people. Kids and parents have been trying to work at home. It is very hard to stop Covid. China started it because some people in China have been eating bats.

Lockdown Memories

Fabian Bell Class 5

In lockdown I went on some walks around Lymm dam. I saw my family and my nannas dogs and had tea there sometimes. We went on holiday to Venezuela and stayed there for 10 days. We mostly stayed in the pool as soon as we got back from holiday. My cousin slept over for a night and had lots of fun. We ate lots of sweets then we dropped her off. But then we had to stay in for 2 weeks because after you come back from holiday you have to stay in so we just got a take away and we ordered calzone. It was really nice.

In lockdown we stayed in quite a bit but we had fun playing board games and reading. Every morning we did Joe Wicks workout in the lounge. It was really fun. Also me and my sister had trampoline challenges. I stayed home playing video games in my room. But we also had a water balloon fight with my next door neighbour. I went to go on the trampoline but then they came running over and threw them at me. I was really cold but then I got my water gun and sprayed them.

We went on a lot of bike rides and tried out the new electric scooter that my uncle had in his car when we went to my nannas to have a barbeque all my cousins were there it was really fun we all had a big water fight on the field with cups because we had no water guns. Me and one of my cousins went into the forest and saw a grass snake slithering in the grass.

My dad and my sister and I went on a hike in the forest and saw a fox. We went over a river but there was no bridge. We had to climb a tree to get to the other side. My sister just went over the stones but they were slippery so she fell in and got wet. The next day we went to climb a mountain. It was really hard when we got to the top we had soup and a whippy walnut it was really nice.

Lockdown Memories

Lacey Breeze Class 5

I remember…

Near the end of lockdown me and my sisters were getting bored so my dad said that we could go to the Lake District for a day. But when we were driving it took nine hours to get there. But actually we went to Somerset Minehead for five days. So while we were there we went to the beach and the city centre. It was very fun. While we were there we went in the pool and sometimes we even went to shows. One night we went to the beach and watched the lighting. It was very pretty.

Right after I went to Butlins my nana and dumps took me and my sisters to Wales for a week. The first day we got there it was raining but we still went on a walk to explore. When we were walking back it was pouring it down. At the night there was really bad wind. So I was up really late and that night my mum and dad slept over. They had to sleep on the sofa bed. The day after my mum and dad went back to our house because they both had work. But we still had fun. On one of the nights we went to a pub. It was very fun because we played chase the ace.

In July we always used to go on walks with my dog called Magic. She is a chocolate labrador and she's very cute. But I always used to check the time because I always went a zoom call with Bethan, Ellie, Lulu and Isla but there's so many other people. I remember when I always used to walk or bike ride to my grandmas. I sat outside with my great nana that asks the same question every minute. She tells stories that aren't even true. Its because she's very old and she's 92 years old.

Lockdown Memories

Maggie Clair Class 5

I loved lockdown because I had a brilliant birthday weekend. Luckily my birthday was two days before my birthday so my friends threw me a social distances party. We walked on the road for hours on end. We camped in the back garden whilst toasting marshmallows on the campfire. Mine got burnt a lot of times. On the day of my birthday I got so many presents that I couldn't fit any more in my wardrobe. For my cake I had Colin the Caterpillar, my favourite. My lockdown birthday was amazing I truly loved it.

My lockdown holiday
My favourite holiday was when I went to the caravan in Northumberland. I loved seeing all the Roman towns. But of course I loved walking along Hadrian's wall. We didn't get to walk along all of it because some of it had sunk into the ground over time and it is very long! We nearly went to the beach every day. Luckily there was an ice cream shop next to the beach so we also nearly got an ice cream every day. But my all time favourite day was when we went to Beamish.

Beamish is an outdoor museum showing about five or six different periods of time. Yep, it was the best holiday I've ever had.

Lockdwn Memories

Eva Corlett Class 5

Beach Day:

I remember when we went on holiday to Wales and we went to the beach. I slipped on the sand and landed on a really pretty seashell. The holiday house was on the beach so I quickly put it in my pocket and when we went home I put it in my bedroom. My dog wriggled SO much while we got the leash off but the other was just sitting there like what is going on! In mine and my sisters room there was a really pretty red heart on the wall made out of seashells! It was as red as the queen of hearts dress! Couple hours later it was bedtime!

Play Park Day:

The next day we went to a play park and there were jumping pillows, dragon slide, a maze, golf, tennis, gokarts and so much more. My fav was the gokarts. I went zooming through the path way and didn't even crash! We went on the jumping pillows first! I got flung off by my annoying brother. Next we went to the tennis/ baseball nets! I was kinda bad at it but I tried and had fun. Then we went on the REALLY fun and scary dragon side. My sister nearly got her leg stuck! We went back to the holiday house and we just relaxed until tea-time I ordered pasta with AMAZING chips. Before you know it its bed-time.

Zoo/Farm Day:
Rise and shine! It's the third day already! Today we are going to the zoo/farm place. When we arrived I saw giraffes, red pandas, lions, turtles, a wild dog, monkeys, all sorts of birds, penguins and so much more. It took a lot of walking but we had but we had so much fun. After we had finished looking at the zoo animals we went to the farm part! I saw baby goats, owls, hens/chickens, cows, pigs and so much more! After we finished looking at all the animals we went to the fair. After the fair we went to the holiday house. My dad came back with his whole body covered in sun burn. He looked like hulk's girlfriend or as my mum said hulk hulk smash smash!

Lockdown Memories

Harrison Dyas Class 5

Throughout lockdown we have been on many walks. On some we got lost. On one we ended up in a field of cows. This was the same one where we had planned to go 4 or 5 kilometres but ended up going 8 kilometres. Almost twice as far as we planned to go. It was extremely annoying to have to walk for about the same amount of time as the school day. When we got back I decided to get onto the Joe Wicks stream to work out and get fit. It was okay but I really didn't like going 8 kilometres when we were only supposed to go 5 kilometres.

On my birthday we had lots of sweets like the old-fashioned cola cubes. Just before this we ate chocolate cake. Later I used my gifts. I was reading while eating cola cubes. After that I watched some animations on YouTube. It was while I was in the middle of a video I realised that there was an extra egged pizza slice. It had the yolk of the egg on the pizza. I went to go get it and ate it whilst finishing my video. After I had the pizza I noticed that there was some cheese so I cut it and ate a piece.

We did some sports in lockdown as well such as football,

basketball and golf. Football was my favourite sport of the three. Sometimes me and my dad would go out running. Other times me and my family would go out for a walk. Golf was okay. It was a bit boring but at least I was getting active. Basketball was my least favorite but it was okay there was nothing bad about it. It is just one of those sports that I don't really like that much but it is still a good sport.

Lockdown Memories

Bea Gowland Class 5

Things I loved and missed

I loved spending time with my family, as I did school work. I liked taking my dog Honey for walks. The thing that I really enjoyed was when covid-19 got a bit better my friends Ellie and Nell invited me to their horse riding party. I got to ride Gemma at Lymm riding school or as most people call it {Rebecca's} riding school. We got to have lots of film nights and my mum made her special homemade toffee popcorn. I liked that I got to still talk to my friends on zoom. Best of all I got to annoy my brother Ben. Me and my family also made vegetable beds and grew herbs, vegetables and sun flowers.I liked clapping for the NHS on Thursdays. I liked doing Jo Wicks every morning, especially on dress up day.

Things I liked and didn't like

I did not like the fact that I had to stay 2m away from other people, especially from the people that I care about the most. I also did not like that I could not see my friends face to face, I missed playing with my friends. I also missed a lot of gymnastics. I did not like that I had to do a lot of school. I especially missed seeing the teachers.

Lockdown Memories

Ellie Gregory Class 5

R is for relaxing reading in a tree
A is for amazing games with my brother
I is for investigating around the house
N is for new books to read
B is for being busy in the house
O is for outside in the garden
W is for walking with my dog and my family.

My Lockdown Memories

Jake Harrison Class 5

I remember...
Doing family runs every morning, having to turn back on myself every 5 minutes because my mum was running as slow as a snail. Making and eating my tasty apricot flapjacks after a brilliant lunch. Finishing my school work by 11oclock and winning the Champions League 10 times on FIFA in the afternoon. Doing 20k bike rides to Dunham Massey Ice Cream Farm. Helping my dad in the garden, cutting the grass. Playing games at night for what seems like all day. Eating delicious melting chocolates. Doing intense football sessions with my dad and brother. Recording football shows and not watching any of them. Buying myself another Match Of The Day subscription although I hadn't finished my first one and got 2 magazines per week.

Having late nights due to film nights and scoffing down sweets and chocolate. Doing Joe Wicks workouts at 9 to 9:30. Online lessons with half of the class and Mr Adams. Toby, my brother, stomping and screaming into my room like a rampaging elephant. Wolfing down delicious meals made by my mum. My mum like sausage casserole. Meeting up with my Nana and Gramps at a peaceful park. Watching Aston Villa losing time and time again until they got 7 points from the last 3 games and stayed up by a point. Trips to my Grandads house, eating crisps and biscuits whilst drinking orange juice. Going to Devon for a few nights and getting fish and chips. Reading Harry Potter until 9 at night with my mum. Going on the Ipad whilst my mum was in the shower, not doing my work.

I CAN'T WAIT FOR THE YEAR 2021 WHEN THERE WILL HOPEFULLY BE NO COVID 19!

Lockdown Memories

Maria Harrison Class 5

I remember when I came home from my grandmas and I got an adorable little puppy named Xena (probably the cutest German Shepherd I have ever seen, no offense to my cat!) On the bright side my cat has company and can have a friend!

I also remember when I went to the best country ever (Poland) in my car (to stay safe) and we had to keep constantly stopping in EVERY country because we brought the dog with us and we stopped and the most stinkiest fuel stations Costa ever had! (What I mean here is that it was in a grotesque state and the bathrooms stunk!) BUY COSTA COFFEE NOW since I don't want Costa to hate me for mentioning them in a bad way!

I remember when I finished the most brilliant game in the world - The legend of Zelda breath of the wild, it took me exactly three years to complete it and yes it was SO hard to do, now we wait for Legend of Zelda breath of the wild 2! How long till it comes out Nintendo?

Lastly I remember when my dad ordered Bhaji Fresh one night and I had delicious, creamy Chicken Tikka Masala (an indian food) and I managed to eat 2 portions of it as I was that satisfied with my meal! Along with that I was hungry and I had only eaten a small bowl of cereal for breakfast that day.

Lockdown Memories

Will Harrison Class 5

I remember...

It was 3 weeks into lockdown me and my family went for a walk. We went down Oughtrington Lane and back and went over to a farmers field and stroked some horses me and my mum stroked them on the nose it did a big nay at us it was funny. We went back home but on the way home me and my family had to go though 2 fields the first one was a field with horses that one was funny because the horses thought we were feeding them so every one of them came over to us. The 2nd one was a manure field with a combine harvester and we had to walk through it.

It was 2 months into lockdown and we decided to go to the airport to see some airplanes. We saw some 7 triple 7s and some 787 air force livery planes. So we were going around the airport for 40 minutes. I was getting tired. I asked my dad how many miles we walked. He said we walked 3 miles and still have 3 miles to go. 6 miles I said we are only used to 2 miles in lockdown. We got to the car and I fell asleep.

3 months into lockdown me and my mum went to go for

a walk with Ben Lubbock and his little brother and his mum around Dunham Massey. It was going well until we found a river that me and Ben could jump over. Me and Ben jumped over the river and back. Ben's little brother tried and got stuck on a branch in the river. Ben jumped in like spider man and his shoe went into the river I jumped and my foot went in the river. My mum told me and Ben off!

Lockdown Memories

Lulu Horner Class 5

At the start of lock down I was worried that I would get bored with the things that we had to entertain me, the drawing, lego, board games. I soon found out that I was wrong as lock down started to loosen...

On my birthday, I discovered that I had got a raised bed and we built it in the front garden. I had a lot of fruits and vegetables to plant. These included kale, strawberries, blueberries, cauliflower, mange tout and green beans. Once the raised bed was finished, we went back to normal lockdown. As time went by, we experienced the progress of the plants. They grew leaves, flowered and produced lots of fruit. All of these vegetables helped us save a lot of money, and I was very grateful for them! Many of the plants produced more fruit than we expected.

Later, it was July, and I was about to climb Pen-y-ghent! As I set off with mum and gran, we began to fall into step with the pitter-patter of the rain. The wind increased too, and soon we were swaying and stumbling along the path up the mountain. When we got to the top I stood on top of the checkpoint, and was nearly blew off by the raging forces of the air. Whilst climbing down the mountainside, the rain and winds calmed down (sort of). After we came back down, I had a massive hot chocolate with whipped cream, that had triple the amount my mum had, along with a huge marshmallow. I was glad that it was over, but I had lots of fun doing it!

Lockdown Memories

Ethan Inskip Class 5

I remember when it was so hot me and my sisters played in the paddling pool. We put the slide on our slip and slide and went super far. We put the slide in the paddling pool and slid down. I went on our trampoline and put the sprinkler under so water sprayed out in between the tiny holes. When it was hot we ate outside (I made some delicious meals!). When it was sunny we went on long walks in spud wood.

I remember in lockdown when I went on my first 5k run with my mum. Me and my dad went on 20k bike rides every night whatever the weather. I played homemade crazy golf with my family and proper golf on my own. Every day at 9:00 am I did PE with Joe, my mum and my sisters. On some nights I made meals like chicken korma and burgers from a Joe Wicks recipe book.

I remember painting rainbows to put on the gate outside my house. I remember painting Lymm rocks, hiding them and finding them (I was the best at finding them)! Every Tuesday at 11:00 am for 1 hour me and my sisters did an online craft club. Every Thursday night at 8:00pm me and my family went outside and clapped for the NHS. I remember planting vegetables and fruit. My favourite was mange-tout.

Lockdown Memories

Lucy Jolley Class 5

I remember ...
Swimming in the paddling pool, chilling in the sun, making funny dances and trying to keep myself busy. Being annoyed by my little sister, playing with the pets and getting dirty in the garden with mum. Stealing my sister's phone and hiding it, then going on night time walks. Sending notes to my friends, doing the dirty work in my pets hutch. Missing my birthday with my friends, my sister moaning at me because she didn't get a birthday video like me. Zooming my family at night and doing quizzes, making dens and helping dad do jobs at home.

I remember...
Watching films with my older sister, playing games with my younger sister, face timing my baby cousin. Meeting up with my bff and getting a Starbucks! Going to her house and her coming to mine for tea and then going crazy after. Having a street party for VE day and eating ice cream whilst chilling outside because we had a heatwave. Doing Joe Wicks before doing home schooling.

Lockdown Memories

Oscar Klendjian Class 5

During lockdown I slept in my back garden in my huge big blue tent. We slept in it for 9 weeks and sometimes my cat slept in it too. But when we took the tent down we had no grass so I couldn't play football but that didn't matter now I could go to the park a lot. The park is really fun and my dad always did shooting. In lockdown I also got my Nintendo switch. It was the best day of my life! Also that day I didn't go to sleep, I just played my switch. When I felt bored I would ask for my mum's phone and then I would go on zoom and talk to all my friends. We basically did it everyday.

Also my mum would organize that I would go to the park at the same time as my friends but social distance. My mum would also organize it so me and my friends could go on a day out, but again at social distance. I also did a lot of my school work. I thought home schooling was better than normal school! Sometimes me and my friends go to the park and play football and do crossbar challenge at social distance.

Book Memories

Alex Ktistis Class 5

I remember reading a lot of books like Magnus Chase, nine from the nine worlds and Percy Jackson and Greek heroes. Nine from the nine worlds has a lot of stories in it and all of them have characters from the Magnus Chase series including Odin, Thor, Sam(Loki's daughter and valkyrie), Hella and Tomas Jefferson junior. In Percy Jackson and the Greek Heroes it has a few Greek myths that include heroes like Perseus, Jason and Otrera. I also read Artemis Fowl and the Arctic Incident. In Artemis Fowl and the Arctic Incident, Lower Elements Police (LEP) ask Artemis Fowl to help them catch Mulch Diggums the dwarf that stole a lot of their money and in return they promised to help him find his father who was captured by the Mafia.

My Lockdown Memories

Ewan Langley Class 5

What I did during lockdown:
I did physiotherapy and speech therapy with Emily.

What I liked during lockdown:
I liked playing with Megan and doing physiotherapy in my hot tub.

What I didn't like during lockdown:
I didn't like doing Maths.

What I missed the most during lockdown:
I missed my friends!

Lockdown Memories

Sophie Lewis Class 5

I remember on my birthday all the wonderful presents I got and was so grateful for. Also one of my best friends (Ruby) came and held up a banner from out of the car window which had all of my favourite things on. One of my other friends (Jess) came and held up birthday bunting in the front garden. For dinner I had Elmas, which is a pizza restaurant and serves yummy food, and my parents surprised me with a tasty cake. Despite all of the restrictions that was a very special birthday.

When the restrictions eased we went on holiday with some friends. Me and my friends made a very fun and funny chicken dance to the Benny Hill theme tune that everyone enjoyed. As the extraordinary house was by the ocean, we went bodyboarding almost every day. There weren't many waves, but that didn't stop us from having fun! The beach was by a big ice cream parlour ,which had many yummy flavours, so we went out and had ice cream. I think everyone who we went with had at least one ice cream from there and loved it. That was a fun holiday with lots of laughs.

We watched a lot of exciting films as a family during

lockdown. On our second holiday, which was just my family, we watched two of the exciting hobbit films. My family, who loves wildlife and adventures, loves animal documentaries and we watched a lot of them during lockdown. My two favourites were bears about the house and John Bishop's great whale rescue. I love watching films with my family.

During lockdown I got to practise and do lots of sporting activities. My dad paid for me and him to become a member of Lymm tennis club. About once a week we would go to the tennis club and play some tennis for about an hour, which was very fun and exciting. I think this has really helped me improve my tennis. Also I went to some red ball lessons and I think that has really helped me remember the basics. Since I have a trampoline in my back garden I have been going on that a lot and I have really mastered a lot of moves but there is always room for more improvement! I have been getting my dad to come on the trampoline with me (and luckily he has been coming on) and we made up this really fun thing where he flings me up in the air as high as the tree tops and I do a straddle jump and when I land I do a seat drop and come back up. I think I have really improved my sport during lockdown.

Lockdown Memories

Isla Loxham Class 5

In lockdown it was my birthday. I had a lovely day with my family because we did some of my favourite things. My mum put in a lot of thought and tried to make it as special as possible. We had a Harry Potter theme breakfast with pancakes and maple syrup. For lunch we had a lovely walk in spud wood with a yummy picnic by the canal. It was my favourite memory in Lockdown.

One of my other memories is that we bought an allotment in lockdown so we grew lots of different things. That meant we did a lot of lovely food like beetroot brownies and scrumptious crumbles. I loved to see the progress of the plants and what they did as they grew. Me and my sister planted lots of seeds and sometimes snuck a blackcurrant in our mouth.

In lockdown we did some fun baking. My dad set me a challenge that was like I was in bake off and I had 1 hour to make over the rainbow cupcakes. It was fun and they were very tasty to eat. My sister did not help because she kept on eating the buttercream but luckily I still had enough! The piping was not the best but they still looked good enough to eat.

I Remember When

Ben Lubbock Class 5

I remember when we walked around the block every day and it got a bit boring after 2 months.

I remember when I got a wonderful new Chris Boardman bike and rode it faster than my Dad.

I remember when I walked to Isaac's house and we played football in the road it was really fun.

I remember when me and Will went on a walk around Dunham Massey and I spider-jumped into Shrek's swamp and just stopped my brother from falling in.

I remember when my brother threw Will's jumper into Shrek's swamp. It was really funny.

I remember that I really enjoyed my first football game back after a long lockdown.

Lockdown Memories

Bethan Marrington Class 5

When we went into lockdown, one of the first things we did was make sure we could talk to friends and family. We used Skype and Zoom. We used Skype to talk to my Nan, Grandad and Jess. We used Zoom to talk to other friends.

There were quite a few hot days in lockdown and we made sure we had lots of fun. Every morning on a hot day, me and my brother Rhys made a den. We did this for shade and one of my dogs (Skye) used it alot, because she is a black dog and gets super hot. We had lots of fun in the paddling pool and had lots of water fights (My mum didn't like these).

In April, it was my Mum and Dad's tenth anniversary and my brother and I dressed up as waiters. It was one of the only days that we were helpful. Lucky for my Mum and Dad, my brother and I got along all day long. For tea we had a takeaway from The Wheatsheaf and it was delicious! Mmmmmmm

One of the most popular things that we did in lockdown was board game Olympics. Sadly, I only won once. To play board game Olympics, you need five games and a table (as in the diagram table not a table that you eat on). You play all the games and whoever wins the most games, wins.

The thing that we did the most of was riding. First we mucked out the fields with the Wrights. We talked and worked for hours until we had to go home. Luckily at the end we always got a snack and a drink. We also had lots of pony days which is when you help out at the stables for six hours and get to ride twice. On a Sunday in lockdown, I had my lesson and helped out on the yard. But then I got a second. I am glad I got that second, because that pony (whose name is Galaxy) is now my loan pony. Loan means that you mainly look after that pony, but it doesn't belong to you. I also got to jump my favourite pony Toby for the first time.

Lockdown Memories

Ned Martin Class 5

Since we were stuck in our house and couldn't go camping. We camped in our lounge for one night. I brought my covers, pillow, blanket and teddy's downstairs then I got comfy and watched BGT, Ninja Warrior UK then in for a penny in for a grand with my family. Then halfway through me and my sister got chocolate muffins, ice cream and a load of fruit. The fruit included an orange, apple, banana, blackberries, strawberries, raspberries, grapes and blueberries. I also sat on my own sofa and made a bed using all the stuff I had. Also we started a new series called Titan Games presented by The Rock (Dwayne Johnson). My mum went asleep halfway through then when it finished I went to bed.

We did a few sport competitions including ping pong, mini golf and family Olympics. Annie won family Olympics and mini golf. Alsol my Dad won ping pong. I came 3rd in family Olympics and mini golf, I came 2nd in ping pong. For family Olympics in each competition you got 4 points for 1st, 3 points or 2nd, for 3rd and 1 point for last (4th) then we added all the points together to see who won. My sister came 1st, my Dad came 2nd, I came 3rd and my mum came last. For mini golf we did the same scoreboard and everyone came the same place on the scoreboard. In ping pong everyone played everyone first to 11. You got 1 point for a win and 0 points for a loss. My Dad won, I came 2nd, my Mum came 3rd and my sister came last.

Lockdown Memories

Reuben Pridding Class 5

I remember when I had a burger the size of my head at the Headland hotel in Cornwall.

I remember going to Blackpool South Pier and eating 4 donuts and not being able to sleep (I can't tell if that's a good memory or not!).

I remember making 2 films (not public) a Imovie, a Inshot.

I remember when my friend, Harrison, live streamed me being bad at Fortnite one time. That was funny!

I remember when I stroked a pig. I didn't think I would ever type that (and that's typing something because I've typed some things!).

I remember when I rode a plastic tractor down a hill and hit a building and put a dent in the fake bonnet.

I remember when my uncle bought a Tesla and it malfunctioned and hit a building and knocked down the whole wall.

I remember when I went golfing and my friend broke 3 tee pegs.owing a treat through the hoop but instead of my dog jumping through she went around it (some people say mannequins will take

I remember when I tried teaching my doggo Mabel to jump through a hoop by throwing a treat through the hoop but instead of jumping through it, she went around it! Some people say that mannequins will take over the world, I say dogs will take over the world because they have a big brain.

I remember doing Joe Wicks every morning.

Lockdown Memories

Silas Pryers Class 5

I remembered when I played Seven Nation Army to my family and Smoke On Water. I remember when I was in my paddling pool with my family and splashing around and having fun with them.

I enjoyed doing online lessons and talking to my friends. I loved it when my friends came and facetimed me and I could talk to them. I liked it when I got all my lessons finished and I could play games on my Switch. I played a little bit of scrabble with my family.

It was epic when friends were allowed to come to our houses and play in the garden. It was fun when I got to see my Godbrothers and father and mother. When I went down the TransPennine Trail with my family and bumped in to one of my friends and had a little chat. When I got home It was really sunny and me and my family went into the freezer and got ice lollies and ice cream.

The best memory I had was when I went to a hotel with my family and I went into the swimming pool and playing croquet. The best bit was when I had calamari for dinner and when we played ping pong (table tennis). I also enjoyed going in the forest near the hotel with my sister. I liked it when we finished our dinner, me and my sister were allowed to go and play croquet or table tennis (ping pong).

My Lockdown Memories

Isaac Richards Class 5

Every morning I did Joe Wicks in my lounge for his live streams. I even bought a t-shirt from his online shop. It is so cool and will definitely be a good memory to have. It was really fun and I loved fantasy dress up Friday. It was hard but I felt better after I had done his daily live streams and loved giving him support.

I facetimed my Nannie and Papa who live in Spain and even celebrated some of my family's Birthdays through zoom. My Grandma lives in Lymm so ring ring, get on the bikes and start riding down the Trans Pennine Trail! Were on our way Grandma! We flew down the trail like lightning.

We went on walks down the canal and had a laugh even nearly having a bath. They were fun and every time we got back my main question was "Please may I have a snack?" I never wanted to go out for a walk but when I got out I found it fun! I'm proud of my family because we're getting fitter.

I went out into the garden making a goalkeeping area for my Dad and I to train in. We had to dig the apple tree out and turn the soil, then finally put in the seed but it didn't work.

My Dad had to buy turf and it worked, Now it looks awesome and will help me with my football. Especially my goalkeeping!

Lockdown Memories

Ariana Roberts Class 5

I remember ...

When lockdown began, I was scared and sad I
would be home all alone.

We adapted to our homes and had play dates
on zoom.

School wasn't school any more.

It was home school!

My mum had a coffee every day and Brenda a
large camomile tea.

Every Thursday we clapped to the NHS.

I collected pots and pans to bash them very
hard .

On VE day we made lots of bunting and hung
them up outside .

Joe Wicks was our PE teacher.

It was a blast!

We went on lots of bike rides in Marbury.

I remember...

When lockdown began, I was sacred and sad I would be home all alone.

Lockdown Memories

Archie Rush Class 5

F is for family. I will always remember when
I'd invite my cousins round for a BBQ and
tell them to jump into the pool. Although it
was boiling hot, the pool was freezing!
A is for always. Always clapping for the NHS
for helping us.
M is for my. For my birthday, I got a brand new
bed and bedroom. It's so cool!
I is for I. I really missed talking to Ben L and
Will H, but as my mum was doing zoom
dancing lessons, I would be on my xbox
speaking to Will and Ben.
L is for losing. As the restrictions got lower, we
all started playing football again and we
kept on losing sadly. But now we keep on
winning.
Y is for yoghurt. Me and my mum would
always go to Yogberries in Hale. We'd both
get frozen yoghurt with delicious toppings

such as brownies with strawberries and oreos. It's so tasty.

Lockdown's Not All Bad

Benjamin Shaw Class 5

A touch of restrictions,
Doesn't stop fun,
It leads to more time with your mum,
Lockdown's not all bad.

When days get hot,
Out we go,
Into the paddling pool we flow,
Lockdown's not all bad.

When weathers bad,
The crafts come out,
So let's make a origami sprout,
Lockdown's not all bad.

When we're bored,
Let's make a play,
We might make it about our day,
Lockdown's not all bad.

When we can't go abroad,
Lets go to Gran's,

She won't mind a extra pair of hands,
Lockdown's not all bad.

Lockdown Memories

Emma Thornton Class 5

I remember that every sunny day I would have to go outside and ride my bike on the road. So that is how I got bored of lockdown and riding my bike. I was practically riding my bike every day! On the plus side of things I would always on hot, sunny days get the paddling pool out. Quite a lot of times, I would go on bike rides with my daddy and sister. Although I got bored of riding my bike on the road, it wouldn't on bike rides because it would be with my daddy.

I also remember that I went on fun runs with my mummy, which were very fun. I love running with my mummy because she is so fun. Funnily enough I bumped into one of my friends from my school. It was when I was running across the swing bridge in Warrington that I saw my friend in her car. We waved at each other and said hello (well we mouthed hello at each other). When I go on the fun runs with my mummy we always go on 5K's which are very fun.

Whilst it was lockdown, I also had my birthday. It was a really good one and it was dinosaur themed which I love. When it was the night before my birthday I didn't get to sleep till 9:00 pm! I celebrated my birthday with my mummy, daddy and sister and my sister drew a cute face for me which was me. We had great fun together because we went to the park and played a game called monster with my daddy which me and my sister made up. In the evening we went out for tea to a place called The Springbrook. It was lovely. I had such a great day!

My Lockdown Memories.

Nell Watt Class 5

I remember when lockdown came. It made me sad because I really wanted to see my friends but I couldn't, so I stayed at home. I didn't like lockdown because it was on my birthday, I wanted to have a good life but lockdown came and ruined it. I wish I could have gone to the shops and Golden Square.

When lockdown calmed down a bit my family went outside and we rode our bikes on the Trans Pennine Trail. It was so much fun and I went horse riding and that was even more fun than riding a bike. We did rainbows for the NHS, we clapped for the NHS, I got some pots and pans and I banged them together. It began to look like it wasn't lockdown at all!

Everybody wanted to have a normal life and not to be in this mess, they wanted to enjoy the whole world.

Lockdown Memories

Jessica Wright Class 5

I remember going down to the stables to muck out the fields. Whenever we were allowed I would finish my work early so that I could go down to Lymm Riding School and help by poo-picking the fields (not by hand of course). Sometimes we would go with friends while socially distanced. I always enjoyed it more if we went with friends but it was still good if it was just me, Mummy and my sister. When Lockdown was eased I started having lessons again with my family. I also started riding more often and I improved a lot. I would go once a week and it was so much fun. Finally, we were allowed to have lessons with friends again, it was really exciting and I loved it so much.

Another thing that I remember is Mummy's birthday. What happened was that a friend was dropping a present off when another friend came up the drive. Mummy opened both presents and was very pleased with them. Next we set up some deckchairs socially distanced in the front garden. We all sat down but suddenly it started raining, so we all put our umbrellas up. Soon after it stopped and we could get back to our conversations. After a while, Daddy brought out the birthday cake that we had made the day before. We all started singing happy birthday but suddenly the candles were blown out by the wind. Then one of my friends shouted, "There's 1 left, there's 1 left" and we all started laughing! It was a great evening.

My Lockdown Diary

Ollie Anderson Class 6

Dear Diary,

I am writing a different diary today. It's about the whole of lockdown and what I did. I am not going to give any clues away about what I did. All I can say is it was an incredible time!

My favourite family memory was when we did an amazing colour baking challenge. This meant we randomly picked a colour. Then we had to make some sort of food using only ingredients that were that colour. Me and my dad got yellow and we made a delicious banana cake with custard and yellow sprinkles. My mum and my brother made a salad with green sweets inside as they got green. To be honest it tasted pretty good. My half brother came round for lunch and he was the judge. And guess what we won!!

My funniest memory was when me and my friend, Alex, went to a place called the Bog of Doom! Unfortunately it was rainy but that made it better. We followed the stream while our parents chatted. Then we found a giant water whole. So of cause we jumped in! We got soaked. When my brother canon-balled, in his fit-bit came off. Me, Alex and my brother dived down in search of the fit-bit. Fortunately we found it and it still amazingly it still worked. After all that we got a bit chilly so we had some warm, bubbling hot chocolate. Our parents were gobsmacked at how dirty we were.

During lockdown me and my dad went fishing quite a bit. One day we decided that we would go fishing. So we got our rods and set off. When we got there some people gave us some wiggly maggots as bait. They were gross! We hooked the maggots and casted out. My brother was first to cast out and guess what. The float sank. He started wrealing in. In the end it was only a small perch. After about five or six casts I caught one. Once again it was perch. I helped my dad unhook it and then we carried on. That morning we caught loads but they were only tiddlers. At lunch time my dad called me and my brother because he had finally got a big carp on the line. Unfortunately it broke off. By the end of the day the biggest fish we caught was no bigger than my hand but it was still fun.

Another thing I did during lockdown is that I learned that I was good at DIY. I found this out when my brother wanted to make a wooden sign to go on his bedroom door

Lockdown Poem

Amalie Aspinall Class 6

L ockdown.
O n a law.
C lap every week for the NHS
K ids of key workers at school
D own the road not a car in sight
O nline lessons
W ith my family at home
N HS you are such a SUCCESS

My Lockdown Diary

Izzy Barnes Class 6

Dear diary,
As I think back to my favourite memories in lockdown, I realised I really developed my baking skills. I would find a recipe and work for hours to make the perfect sweet treat for my family and friends. I made chocolate cake,caramel cake, tiffin, chocolate orange biscuits, chocolate chip cookies, scones and chocolate meringue slice. Every time I baked something, I delivered some to my elderly neighbours, so they could try my sweet treats.

My favourite family memory was VE Day, when everyone sat in their gardens and had afternoon tea. My friends and I were out on the street chatting, playing, painting and riding our bikes whilst social distancing. My family and I put blue and white bunting in the garden and coloured in pictures of the Union Jack to put in the window.

My funniest memory was when I watched a movie called Ace Ventura: Pet Detective with my family. Some parts of the movie were so funny, my brother and I fell off the sofa laughing. We now have family movie night every Saturday.

In lockdown, I learned that I really like spending time with my brother. We made shows on the trampoline, slept in a two person tent in his room, made dens out of sheets and blankets, played with the guinea pigs and played volleyball and football.

I wonder what tomorrow will bring?

NHS Rule

Georgia Breeze Class 6

We have been in history,
And Covid-19 will be a mystery.
I hope the NHS,
Has all the success.
People fund raise,
And people praise.
The news,
Gets lots of views.
6 months of homeschool,
We can't even go in a pool.
We can treasure,
And share memories together.
Put a rainbow in your window,
To show your appreciation.
My families hearts,
Fell apart.

My Lockdown Diary

Sophie Burke Class 6

Dear diary,

Today I am writing in my diary but not about today but what happened in lockdown. Lockdown was bitter-sweet. As I look back I remember one of my funniest memories.

I was on a walk with my family and we found a beautiful waterfall. It was like a dream. There were lots of other waterfalls there too. Me and my sister went in the river and got our feet all wet. Then we saw an amazing waterfall. The water rushed over the rocks and made a calming sound. We were standing at a top of a huge hill and realised that if we wanted to see it properly we would have to go down to the bottom. It was like a straight line, like the ones at the playgrounds. It was very slippery because it rained the night before. We slid down from tree to tree.

As we hit the bottom we were covered in mud. If we wanted to see it properly, we would have to climb over a tree that had fallen over the river. As we were walking back, we found an easier path which we could have walked down! When we got back we went to the cafe and got a bacon butty. It was amazing! We also had a scone with jam and cream and I think we deserved it!!

I will never forget this day. Lets see what tomorrow brings.

I Am The NHS

Bella Byrne Class 6

Everyday,
We slave away.
I appreciate that you fundraise,
You deserve lots of praise.
I can see lots of rainbows,
Brightening up your windows.
Our news,
Got lots of views.
All together,
We will reach the treasure.
We can eat covid-19 for dinner,
And we will be the winner.

I am Family Time

Holly Clarkson Class 6

I am Family Time.
What bothers me most is that we can't see our
friends.
I wish for everyone to stay safe.
I am happy when we watch TV.
What makes me angry is not being able to
leave the house.
I dream of Lockdown being over.
I wish for more Family Time.
I am Family Time.

My Lockdown Diary

Lucas Corlett Class 6

Dear diary,

One Saturday during lockdown, I looked out my window and thought it would be the perfect day to go biking. I went and woke up my family but I didn't expect for them to wake up because it was around eight in the morning. They woke up quite cranky! Well, apart from my brother who was ignoring me. My mum said that we could go for a bike ride when I woke her up. My brother didn't want to wake up at all, so we kept trying for about 1 hour. Finally, he woke up!

At around ten in the morning, we had our breakfast and got our bikes outside standing up against the wall. We were all ready to go! We all checked our bikes with the M Technique. Then we went around Dallam, Bewsey and Westbrook. We were trying to go all the way around Penketh before going back home.

We made a stop at Tesco to get food and a drink. We had to wait for my sister because she was being slow at eating.

When she was finished, we went all the way around again. That was the only quick way back to Widnes North. After about an hour my mum fell over. We helped her up but she walked because we were still 20 mins away. We finally made it home and had a rest!

I had a lot of fun but my favourite part was going out on bikes with my family and being able to get outside!

My Lockdown Memories!

Abi Craig Class 6

Dear Diary,

As I think back to my favourite memories during Lockdown, I realise that I developed a lot of skills. I have a lot more hobbies. I had even started to develop talents I was never interested in and that I never knew I could do! My sports interests have changed a lot over Lockdown (Lockdown was very very fun!). The hobbies that I had developed are; I am much better at typing, I am faster at running, I am better at aiming in netball and I am good at cheerleading.

My favourite family memories are when we used to do Friday night Kahoots. I also loved going to Scotland because we went to a lot of places like Inverness and the Highlands. I loved staying in all different hotels because I came up with the idea of doing a family game of 4 in a bed (the tv show) it was really fun.

Two of my most funniest Lockdown memories are when I

beat my Mum on a nursing Kahoot and she is a nurse (I was just guessing)! Also I beat my Dad on a helicopter Kahoot and he loves helicopters. I also fell off my close friend Bella's trampoline head first and I didn't even hurt my head, I just hurt my shin.

In Lockdown I learned a lot about myself especially that I like watching and doing cheerleading.

Lockdown Memories

Amelie Danby Class 6

Dear Diary,

I remember when I experienced lock down, my funniest memory was when we were doing Joe Wicks. Joe did a lot of abs work so Henry did not enjoy it. He started off fine and was doing all the work outs but he ended up on the floor almost about to cry!

A hobby or talent I developed:
I learned how to cook a naughty chocolate cake - it was delicious! I also did a lot of cooking with my family. We had a lot of burgers and BBQs. Henry and I did a lot of art and I ended up stealing all of the paint!

Something I learned about myself:
In lockdown I tried to get creative so I started to watch craft videos. After watching very carefully, I started to paint. It took a while, but I ended up painting some very realistic and good paintings.

My favourite memory:

At the start of isolation we had a card competition and we played every night. My mum came first, Henry came in 2nd place, I came 3rd and dad came last!

My Lockdown Diary

Alexander Davies Class 6

I remember in lockdown when my family and I went to a place with lakes that you could walk around with my Nana and Grandad. On the way we listened to Alan and Mel. I was very excited because we hadn't seen them in ages. We had talked to them just before we left. I couldn't wait.

When we got there we had to wait, because we were a bit early. As soon as they arrived, we ran over as fast as we could and gave them a big hug (we were allowed to though!). After that, we went for a 2 mile walk around a lake and we saw people waterskiing! We thought it must have been very cold. As we were walking around, I saw some people on go karts that you pedaled and could steer. "Mum, can I have one of those for Christmas please?" I pleaded. About halfway round, we attempted to play frisbee. I said attempted because it turns out it's very difficult to play frisbee in 40 mph wind. When we tried to throw it, it just came straight back to us like a boomerang.

After the frisbee ordeal, we carried on and went round

another lake, back to the playground. After a little trip to the loo, we played on the playground and climbed a very cool tree! It was so cold that we had to go into the car to warm up. My Mum and Grandad said that they would go to the cafe and get us all a hot drink. Yum! After 20 minutes they still hadn't returned so I went to check where they were but as I got near they came out, so I waited for them and walked back with them. I took a big mouthful and swallowed it immediately, as it was insanely hot. I opened it up to let it cool down and there was 50 marshmallows and I'm not even exaggerating!

This was my favourite lockdown memory ever!

I am Lockdown

Jack Doyle Class 6

I solation was difficult.
S ad because we couldn't go out.
O n our own.
L ockdown the country.
A way from friends.
T ime to play games.
I had fun with my family.
O nline learning was fun.
N ow we're back in school.

My Lockdown Memories

Amelia Giblin Class 6

Dear Diary,

When I look back over lockdown, I have many memories but my favourites are...

Our daily family bike rides were so fun and we were always really tired out after them. We would go for miles and stop and have a picnic. I also loved gardening with my mum and dad. I would run into the sprinkler at random times. We went to the caravan with my whole family and went fishing and had a massive barbeque on the beach.

I had loads of fun over lock down but my favourite funny memory was when we went to Gulliver's world with my cousins, my mum, my sister and my auntie. We went on a massive slide and bounced off water. We also went on a boat ride. We soon went home and went to bed very tired out.

I developed many things but mostly I learnt how to do gardening without getting messy! We did our gardening everyday after our bike ride. We had sooooooooooooooo much fun. We all went in the sprinkler and cried laughing.

I learnt that I prefer home schooling and I have the confidence to do more things. I also felt that I could do things at my own pace and finish when I was ready.

My Lockdown Diary

Bethany Gilchrist Class 6

Dear Diary,

It has been a rough time in this pandemic, but there has been some fun times.

Video calling my brother Arthur and my mum because I can't see them very much. Baking yummy cupcakes with my Auntie Molly and arguing over who gets what part. Going on walks with my Nan and my dog Noodles. Kal, my auntie Chloe's baby, was born. My mum bought a fart pillow and caution sign because my brother trumps a lot . Watching funny videos of me and my mum from years ago. Playing a song with my brother and his baby toys and making him laugh lots and lots. Crafting with my big box of paints, brushes, pencils and coloured pencils. Making pictures and sending them to my dad.

I was very impatient when things seemed to take forever. I got really wound up when when my Auntie Molly joked around about me. Aunties these days!

House Lock

Luke Haskins Class 6

As it was very hot weather,
I did my work to make me more clever.
When we went for a walk,
We would always talk.
When there was a rainbow,
I would always look at it through the window.
When we played twister,
I would always get a blister.
As we are in isolation,
I have a very good imagination.
Weekly clapping for the NHS,
To make getting rid of this virus a success.

The Lockdown Town

William Hyunh Jackson Class 6

Segregation of our education,
Confined in our minds to our innovation.
Playing games like toilet-roll,
To control our brain-flow.
Because togetherness is treasure,
Even if we're apart but never in our hearts.
Retreat from the streets,
Exiled is the style,
To protect the NHS for their success.

My Lockdown Memories Poem

Millie Legge Class 6

This is my poem about lockdown,
Some days I had a frown.
Most days I would go for a walk,
Just me and my parents and we would talk.
Some days I was alone,
So all I did was play on my phone.
Over lockdown I made a rainbow,
Just for the NHS and put it in my window.
Because of this dreadful year,
None of us got to cheer.
None of us enjoyed this pandemic,
But luckily we had the medics.
Families bonded together,
As they will, forever.

My Lockdown Poem

James Mayne   Class 6

This is my great poem about being in LOCKDOWN,
Where we have to stay indoors and can't go to TOWN.
Unfortunately we have to stay in ISOLATION,
When I do my homework I use my IMAGINATION.
Me and my family played fun GAMES,
That were good for our BRAINS.
We all clap for the NHS,
Whilst they try and bring us SUCCESS!

I Am The NHS

Aine McAfee Class 6

I am the NHS,

What bothers me most is seeing people slowly suffer and we can't help them,

I wish for Covid-19 to disappear and life to go back to normal,

I am happy when people get discharged from hospital feeling better,

What makes me angry is when people come into hospital and don't need to,

I dream of a time when life is normal and nobody has to stress,

I am the NHS,

I am your support!

I Am Lockdown

Issy Minnery Class 6

I come and go like rapids in the sea,
I may be bad, I may be good,
But it's the best for you and me.
Sometimes people really can't cope,
But you just have to pray and hope.
I keep you stuck in isolation,
But it's fine, it brings out your imagination.
You shout and stress,
It really shows your frustration.
You can slowly brush Covid 19 away,
If you just make a wish today!

My Lockdown Poem

Jess Minnery   Class 6

Lockdown is in everyone's head,
But once it's over we can all get out of bed.
Whilst Covid is giving us hugs,
No-one can walk their pugs.
We all have to work together,
So lockdown won't go on forever.
Covid is all over the news,
Whilst people can't go on a cruise.
I dream of the NHS team,
Beating Covid-19.

Isolation!!

James Perry Class 6

I n isolation it's so boring
S ocialising online is so strange
O ver time more and more die
L iving in lockdown it's so sad
A few people breaking the rules
T he family quizzes were so fun
I n the shop I wear my mask
O n the road there's not a car
N ever alone in my home

I Am Covid-19

Hugh Pridding Class 6

I am Covid-19. I am the virus of the century. I am what all of the news channels are discussing.

I may seem cruel by killing so many humans and even some other animals but that is my way of cleansing the earth and restarting, to turn a new leaf! I wish for everyone to be infected by me so Earth can be like it was millions of years ago when it was a beautiful tropic with glimmering waters and warm breezes, but then those brain-dead apes had to evolve,

What bothers me the most is the fact that some stupid rainbow people think they have a chance! (I am actually quite afraid of them but this is my thoughts, no-one can hear me, right?). But annoyingly they're helping the humans stay happy and healthy and when they catch me, they help them by treating them which is annoying but it does make just a slight bit of sense seeing they're doctors, but still that's the opposite of what I want.

I absolutely love it when people fall into traps I didn't even set surprisingly by throwing parties, not social distancing with people outside of their bubble and not isolating when infected which is great. I love being passed around! I also don't understand it because the NHS is the best hope for the UK and some people still don't follow the rules set by them,

I despise it when the idiots at the NHS (and the countries healthcare systems like Germany) make progress on the vaccine because I know it will fail (at least, I hope it will!) and I have no doubt about that statement (not really). I also despise it when you use hand sanitiser, stinky alcohol ooze, because it makes it harder for me to spread and there's something in that satanic version of soap that I'm allergic to! I'm determined to make sure that the human race becomes extinct...

My Lockdown Diary

Finlay Roberts Class 6

Dear Diary,

My funniest memory that happened in lockdown was when I got invited to Oscar and Sebastian's birthday party at their house. So me and my Mum went to the shop to get them a gift card as a present. Then this is what we did.

Off I went to their house with my Mum. When we arrived, I charged out of the car and round the side of the house into the garden where I could hear everybody shouting and having fun. First, I went over to Oscar and Sebastian's Mum and gave her the present to give to Oscar and Sebastian later. Then I said hello to everyone at the party and joined in with the football. I scored some goals and tackled everyone. I was also going in net a bit and saving some amazing shots that hurt my fingers. Whenever someone scored a goal, everybody cheered. Everyone was very energetic and excited. So was I. Just before lunch we were all being silly, trying to be the one bouncing on the space hopper. That was lots of fun but a bit chaotic!

At lunch, we all sat at the table and had some delicious food. We had all sorts of pizza, dough balls, fries and fizzy apple juice. It was delicious! Then after that we sang happy birthday to Oscar and Sebastian. Then we went to play some more football. Whilst we were playing, one of us kicked the ball very hard and it zoomed towards the table that had glass bottles on it. The ball bounced onto the table and bounced between all of the glass bottles and then bounced off the table and into the bin without breaking a single bottle!

Later we went on these amazing peddle go carts and I was one of the best people at driving them. It was very hard to turn around in the little turn around spot because I only managed to do it once without picking the cart up and turning it around. I also went on the tiny tractor and pulled some some friends around on it. That was one of the most fun parts of the whole party!

When my mum arrived, I didn't want to leave because I was having so much fun. After Oscar and Sebastian had given me a party bag, I happily went home.

My Lockdown Poem

Oscar Spink Class 6

This is my poem about lockdown.
Where we have to stay indoors and cannot go to town.
I feel alone in isolation,
But not in my imagination.
I always play games,
To improve my brains.
I love the NHS,
And wish them success!

Isolation

Sebastian Spink   Class 6

I nside my house I feel safe
S ad people wanting to see their families
O bserving birds is no more
L ockdown has brought us all down
A lone, sometimes feeling lost
T ime to try and fight back for freedom
I n the street one or two people there
O ur hopes have dimmed down
N ow is our time to shine

I Am Lockdown

Maddox Stevens Class 6

Six months off school,
And we couldn't even go in the pool.
We were in isolation,
At least now we have a good imagination.
People breaking the rules, getting caught by police,
There was no peace.
All of us were on our games,
That wasn't very good for our brains.
We have been in quarantine,
Then I was stuck with my teen.
Everyone was watching TV,
That was very easy.
We were all segregated,
All of us were one-on-one educated.
I Am Lockdown!

Lockdown

Laura Swettenham Class 6

We have had to be at home,
But at least we were not our own.
We are spending time happily,
As a great big family.
We can go for a walk,
Or maybe have a talk.
Make a rainbow,
To stick on your window.
Because of this terrible year,
None of us got to cheer.
In lockdown,
We realised that we don't need to go into town.
The house is where we stay,
Though we can still play.
At the start of this year, the pandemic started to appear,
But thanks to the NHS it will slowly disappear.
Now lockdown is over,
We are not in as much risk of exposure.

My Lockdown Diary

Ella Walker Class 6

Dear Diary,

I remember when we were in lock down and my favourite family memory was when we welcomed my Grandpa to our family support bubble. My Grandpa and I both love Chinese takeaways so we decided to get one as it was fathers day and also my mum and dad's anniversary. It was very yummy and the four dogs loved it.

A Hobby I Developed

I spent a lot of time cooking for my elderly neighbours. I made a lot of cakes, biscuits, bread and pizzas. I also spent a lot time on Minecraft building houses. I did art a lot of the time, watching drawing tutorials and using my glue gun. It was a lot of my family's birthdays so I made a lot of cakes - I think I should start a business making birthday cakes!

My Funniest Memory

I had so many funny memories but I think this one is the funniest. We had to make an Imovie for Mr Adams, so I asked my Dad and 2 dogs to help and my brother asked to help too.

I put a tutu on 1 of my dogs and she was Superdog, my brother put a wig on and I wore a bat girl costume. But my Dad went over board! He put on a 1970s costume, a puffy wig and he was a baddy called Disco Dave. It spent the whole dad. But it was really fun we all loved it!

Something I learned about Myself
I really miss school and miss hugging people. And that I miss seeing my friends.